MW01294207

THE LEAN BUILDER

BUILDER

*A Builder's Guide to Applying
Lean Tools in the Field*

**JOE DONARUMO
&
KEYAN ZANDY**

ISBN: 978-1-4834-3093-5 (sc)
ISBN: 978-1-4834-3092-8 (e)

Library of Congress Control Number: 2019910345

Edited by Dara Davulcu
Illustrations by Kaustubh Shukla

Lulu Publishing Services rev. date: 08/12/2019

Praise

Written for those who roll up their sleeves and do the work as craft professionals, foremen, and superintendents, *The Lean Builder* is a must-read for anyone new to Lean Construction, and certainly those professionals working in the field.

Cleverly written as a story with characters anyone in construction can relate to, *The Lean Builder* presents Lean processes, from pull planning and the Last Planner System® to Lean principles such as respect for people and continuous improvement. This book is easy to read and delivers these Lean concepts in a clear and understandable manner through practical scenarios within a construction project team. Any team, even those with individuals not very open to change and too comfortable with the status quo, would benefit from learning the Lean Construction practices and lessons so masterfully explored in *The Lean Builder*.

Michael F. Stark, CAE, IOM
Chief Executive Officer
AWCI - Association of the Wall and Ceiling Industry

Finally, a guide for the front lines! *The Lean Builder* is a must-read for anyone looking to make our industry safer, more productive, and a most desirable place to work. The story teaches readers to see how they, in their daily routines, might leverage the power of teams making small improvements to build trust, reduce stress, and unlock the potential of the most valuable people on our projects—the builders in the field.

As a snapshot of who we are, as well as our potential, I hope *The Lean Builder* inspires current and future builders by empowering the people closest to the work to improve the work. It should be considered a professional development guide that gives us all the courage to embrace the kind of evolution that this relatable story makes real.

Bevan Mace
VP, National Operations and Lean
Balfour Beatty
2017 Lean Construction Institute Chairman Award Winner

One could make a credible argument that the purest, most true value in the construction industry rests in the hands of the least visible, least recognized people in the whole project delivery spectrum—the craft workers in the field. They are the only ones who physically put work in place and the rest of us in the supply chain exist to enable them to do just that. Sadly, we have not given them the focus and attention they deserve. Happily, this book is a massive step in the right direction! Your job is simple:

read this book. Then, get others to read this book. Together, we will transform the industry!

Romano Nickerson, AIA
Principal
Boulder Associates Architects
2014 Lean Construction Institute Chairman Award Winner

To be perfectly honest, I came to this book as a skeptic; but I must confess that something magical happened as I sat down and began to read this story. I believe Keyan and Joe have captured the essence of what we all face during the critical phases of our work. I highly recommend this book to anyone, especially those closest to getting the work done. They will undoubtedly see themselves in Sam, and emphatically connect with his passion, anger, frustrations, goals, and ultimately his success with bringing a project together by applying the Last Planner System. *The Lean Builder* is something worthy of our time—at least, for those builders who are fed up with the B.S. of our traditional construction methods.

Henry Nutt, III
Sheetmetal General Superintendent
Southland Industries
2018 Lean Construction Institute Pioneer Award Winner

The Lean Builder is a friendly read that offers a great interpretation of a few different ways a superintendent can bring Lean and the Last Planner System to their jobsite, and gives a real-life practical application. Materials of this kind are usually geared towards people other than those who are directly responsible for getting projects built in the field. It's refreshing to see this written in a business fable format and geared towards the people who have the day-to-day ability to implement these solutions so closely to where the real value to capital projects is delivered. The openness and transparency that went into the content of the book highlights the authors' drive for a better industry!

Rebecca Snelling
Lean Leadership Coach, Owner
RS Consulting
2018 Lean Construction Institute Chairman Award Winner

●●●

The Lean Builder puts the focus where I believe Lean practices have the biggest impact: with the men and women who do the work. It is easy to identify with the main character, Sam, because I have personally seen this story unfold many times over my forty-two years in the trade. Sam takes us through the numerous, familiar frustrations that are challenges on almost every project, and through his eyes we see how he successfully adapts to real-time constraints through pull planning, team collaboration, trust, and respect.

It's a story that anyone that has been involved on a construction project will see value in reading. I applaud the authors for bringing a simple story instead of a manual to resonate with readers and help them to start (or restart) their Lean journeys.

Greg Stedman
Lean Director
KHSS Contractors

Foreword

by Dan C. Heinemeier and Dick Bayer

I want to congratulate Joe and Keyan for their passion for more effective Lean implementation at the workface, and for producing a book to help make this happen. It's all too common that Lean experts focus on creating thorough, top-flight learning materials, but fail to inspire those who ultimately must make it happen: the superintendents, foremen, and others who guide and oversee project work on a daily basis. In contrast, the authors of this book have created a work that reads more like a novel than an instruction manual.

I predict many "ah-ha" moments as readers gain better understanding of Lean as applied to real work situations. Many will see their own struggles reflected in the experience of the main character, Sam, who stumbles a bit at first but perseveres to see his project transformed. In the process, team members who were shut down and even hostile come around as Sam adopts a new leadership model that gets everyone committed to making it happen. Readers will learn along with Sam how the Lean system becomes self-reinforcing, leveraging the power of collaboration and respect for people to move project teams to ever-greater success.

This is a book that should be read by anybody who sees Lean as too challenging to attempt, and even those who have tried it before and failed. It will correct misperceptions and inspire people to try something new. Hand it out to your project teams and watch the light bulbs come on!

Dan C. Heinemeier
Executive Director
Lean Construction Institute

●●●

I met Keyan Zandy in a trailer. In Dallas. Where recent rains made access difficult. This will sound very familiar to you after you read *The Lean Builder* (and you will read it!)

Production is where the value in construction lies, and your line workers are your trades. Every other thing done on a construction site is meant to facilitate the ability of the trades to install the work. Unfortunately, we have spent years making it as difficult as possible for our trade partners to be successful—we have siloed their contracts, we have given them unrealistic deadlines created by unreliable computer programs, we have tried to get them to work at a faster pace than is fair or reasonable, and we have pitted them against one another in the race for territory and work.

Many of the soft skills and organizational behaviors and tools developed in Lean Construction are aimed at solving those issues. The problem with connecting people to those behaviors is that they are usually demonstrated as part of a slideshow in a rented hotel conference room, and are rarely demonstrated where they belong: at the workface. My friend, Keyan Zandy, and his friend, Joe Donarumo, have finally given us a different tool that speaks to the problems of ordinary job sites and ordinary trade partners who deliver extraordinary work. This field guide for the application of Lean tools in the trailer and on a construction site sets the stage for the exact same problems so many of us have faced when introducing the tools and the concepts, and it offers the perfect prescription at every turn.

As a guy who loves to spend time in trailers with the real teams, I can't wait to share this work with the dedicated men and women who actually build our projects. Thank you, Joe and Keyan!

Dick Bayer
Chairman, the ReAlignment Group
Interim Executive Director Emeritus, Lean Construction Institute
2013 Lean Construction Institute Chairman Award Winner

Preface

If you are reading this right now, we would like to thank you for the opportunity to share our journey and passion for Lean Construction. Our background as Lean practitioners as well as construction operations leaders has afforded us what we feel is a unique perspective on the most effective ways to apply Lean practices and tools in the field.

While many wonderful and insightful Lean design and construction publications exist, our background and passion are focused on field-applied Lean—or *Builder's Lean*, as we call it—which we feel is currently underrepresented in publications. We were motivated to explain the concepts, tools, and principles of Lean in an engaging fable format that also provides insight on the nuances and soft skills that are helpful to effectively implement Lean in the field.

The beauty of Lean is that it is never complete; it is always focused on learning, sharing, and continuous improvement. The implementation of Lean can be challenging because change from the status quo is disruptive. Many have accepted the significant waste that plagues our industry as just part of the job, not recognizing the current state is broken and in desperate need of repair. We must find solutions to reduce waste, improve workflow, and add value for project stakeholders. Field-applied Lean can be that solution.

While we hope that a wide audience enjoys this book and finds it informative and helpful, *The Lean Builder* was written for a specific group of people: the leaders in the field—the superintendents and last planners. Our goal is to provide an easily understood, accessible resource for you so you'll feel empowered to implement Lean methodologies on your projects, even if you have no other resources or champions available to you. We invite you to be open-minded and willing to explore these new ideas and concepts, which may push you to abandon the comfort zone that is "that's the way we have always done it."

Respectfully,
The Lean Builders
Joe Donarumo
Keyan Zandy

Acknowledgments

A book is the sum of many pieces—ideas, perspectives, beliefs—that are assembled not just when the author sits down and starts to type, but over the course of a lifetime. People whom we have known, learned from, worked with, and taught over the years have given us the seeds. These settled into our minds and took root, and in some way have helped to shape what you're currently holding in your hands. In that spirit, we'd like to acknowledge the following people who have played a role in this book's creation.

Keyan Zandy would like to gratefully acknowledge:

First, my wife, partner, best friend, and love of my life, Tere Zandy. You tolerated late nights, lost weekends, and endless dinnertime conversations about this project. Thank you for giving me the time and space I needed to make this dream become a reality.

Stewart Trapino, my old colleague and friend—thank you for adding fuel to my flame for Lean Construction, motivating me, and challenging me to find a way to make the tools scalable so that more people could benefit.

Another old colleague and friend, Jason Becker, who spent countless hours working with me in daily huddles and pull plan sessions. Together, we refined and reshaped Lean tools so they would work their best in the field, and eventually created what we call "Builder's Lean."

My former client and good friend Jeff Schroder, who so deeply values the contributions of individual people and the importance of relationships. He showed me how important the foundations of friendship and trust are in both team-building and in maximizing the efficacy of Lean tools.

My partners, Clay Harrison, Dwayne Hodges, and Brent Brown, who added me to their leadership team, entrusted me with the keys to their firm, and gave me the freedom to guide its direction and shape its culture.

And last but not least, the entire staff at Skiles Group—collectively, you made me both a teacher and a student, and your support has helped me to evolve as a leader. I especially want to acknowledge my "Lean Champion," Buddy Brumley, who trusted me enough to give Lean a chance and quickly became an advocate and mentor to others when I could no longer be a practitioner myself. Together, we implemented the tools and processes that would forever change the way Skiles Group does business, and I couldn't have done it without you.

Joe Donarumo would like to gratefully acknowledge:

My beautiful and talented wife Tasha Donarumo - through your support, friendship, and encouragement, you have enabled me to achieve the things I have set my focus on. I love you with my whole heart. Thank you for your patience, wisdom, and love. I'm so blessed.

My co-author Keyan Zandy and colleague Jason Becker – thank you both for creating the spark and allowing me to grow, share, and create alongside you. I'm very grateful for our journey together!

My mentors at Linbeck, Mark Linenberger and Stewart Trapino – thank you both for helping me understand the power of self-awareness and the impact it can have on a jobsite when leveraged. I'm grateful for your support, honesty, and helping me to realize my "why".

And lastly to Stan Davis and Spencer Seals of Cook Children's Medical Center – thank you for allowing me the opportunity to serve your organization and providing me the platform to grow, create, and refine the skills and processes that enable the last planners to be successful!

● ● ●

And Joe and Keyan would both like to express their deep appreciation for and gratitude to:

Our friend, Romano Nickerson—we appreciate the gift of your advice, wisdom, and friendship. Thank you for validating our content, and especially for helping us get this book off the ground and into the hands of our readers.

And finally, our friend and editor, Dara Davulcu—you patiently nurtured enormous paragraphs of unformatted text into an engaging story with interesting characters. The invaluable contribution of your ideas, imagination, and words made our story richer than we had initially envisioned, and this book wouldn't be what it became without your thoughtful influence.

Table of Contents

Prologue

Sam Brooks closed the door on the back of the moving truck and then turned around to find his wife crying on the sidewalk. It was hard to leave after seven years. Virginia had been good to them; they'd made friends, felt like a part of their community, and had a nice little townhouse they'd grown to love through years of TLC and various improvements. The mountains, the trees, and especially the diversity of seasons had all been novel. But Sam was not going to miss the east coast winters, or especially the snow. "Your blood is just too thin for that place!" his grandmother liked to say, as if that were a real thing people could have. (But when it was below freezing and he was shoveling snow, there was a part of him that wondered if she might be onto something.)

Jen blew her nose. Sam laughed and gave her a hug. "I want to go home," she said, pressing herself to him.

He nodded, hugging her back. "Me, too."

"Home" was Texas. It's where they had both grown up, where they met, and where they had fallen in love, even though Virginia was where they had been married. They met in high school and had stayed together ever since. People doubted that high school sweethearts would stand the test of time, but Jen and Sam knew

better. After their high school graduation, Jen went to college while Sam enlisted in the army. As basic training progressed, Sam's buddies received returned engagement rings in the mail, but Sam never doubted that he and Jen would last. And he was right; throughout his six-year enlistment and two deployments, they were steadfast.

The primary reason they were moving back home was because they were ready to start a family. Admittedly, Jen was more ready than Sam, but he was excited as much as he was afraid. Jen came from a large family and, as far as she was concerned, they had already waited long enough. But Sam only had one younger brother and didn't feel the pull for a bigger family like Jen did. There was a compromise to be found somewhere, and he knew they would find it.

However, they agreed that they both wanted to be closer to their families when they had children of their own. They'd found a small house in a rural bedroom community nearly an hour outside of the Dallas–Fort Worth metroplex. The house needed work (and the addition of more bedrooms, as Jen always said whenever she told people about their new house.) Sam was capable of all of this and looked forward to the projects. But, best of all, there was land. Over five acres, which meant dogs, maybe a couple of horses someday, and a big garden for Jen to play with. Despite her tears, they were both excited to start their next chapter back in their home state.

This type of homestead was very different from the way Sam had grown up. He lived on a tree-lined street in a cozy Dallas neighborhood and attended crowded public schools with hundreds of other kids. He had a lot of friends growing up, but there was only one like Andrew Phillips.

Andrew and Sam met in elementary school and had grown up together on the same street where they lived their entire lives—and where Andrew's parents, Alan and Elsie, still lived. They graduated high school together, and even joined the army together. They were the kind of best friends who spent nights with each other every weekend and burned through entire summers together, from coloring books to camp outs, to driver's licenses, and beyond.

The boys were as much a part of each other's families as their own. Alan took them fishing, corrected their manners, showed them how to change oil and replace the fan belts in their cars, and taught them basic woodworking in his garage. Unlike Alan (who on principle didn't believe in paying his children to do anything), Sam's dad, James, could always be counted on for cash in exchange for odd jobs like staining the fence, washing the cars, or cleaning the gutters. These chores never dried up, and they funded countless trips to ice-cold theaters for dollar movies and a welcome escape from one-hundred-degree days during their long summer breaks.

Even so, if he were honest, Sam preferred being at Andrew's house over his own. Andrew had four older sisters, and Sam found them foreign and entertaining. The house was always buzzing with their laughter, arguments, and energy, and Elsie was always pulling something delicious out of the oven. (For his part, Andrew probably preferred it at Sam's, where there were fewer girls and more quiet.)

Alan worked in construction, which captivated Sam. He had a blast when Alan would take them to his jobsites, let them wear hard hats, and climb on the backhoes and bulldozers. Sam loved watching the progress of the buildings as they came out of the ground and went up into the sky, and he would wear Alan out with his endless questions. He thought the construction process was magically transformative; buildings under construction were constantly changing from one day or week to the next.

This fascination was not something that he and Andrew had in common. Andrew was more interested in animals and biology, looking at drops of pond water under his microscope, and digging for arrowheads and fossils instead of digging to lay a foundation for a new building.

Alan enjoyed Sam's curiosity about his work and nurtured it where he could. The leather tool belt that Alan gave Sam when he turned seventeen was one of his most favorite things. He still had it and looked for any opportunity to wear it—which also provided opportunities for Jen to tease him.

"You're installing a smoke detector in your pajamas, Sam. Aren't you overdoing it?" she'd ask, laughing. He'd solemnly remind her that a man should always come to work prepared.

The boys were so close and spent so much time together that their two homes, only three apart on the same side of the street, seemed blended. Sam and Andrew felt like they'd grown up with two families and two sets of parents. When they left for basic training within a few weeks of each other—first Andrew, who was headed to Fort Benning, and then Sam, who left for Fort Leonard Wood—Sam's mom, Michelle, cried just as hard over Andrew's departure as Sam's, and Elsie crushed Sam against her with as much maternal grief as she'd used when hugging Andrew on the day he had left.

Sam and Jen had traveled back to Texas as often as possible in the intervening seven years, even though it wasn't as often as either of them would have liked. There were births and birthdays, bridal showers and weddings, Christmases and Thanksgivings, and summer trips for no reason. Then there was James's funeral three years ago. And Andrew's, last spring.

Sam had had enough of the army after six years, but Andrew, a combat medic, re-enlisted. Jen had moved to Virginia after graduating college to take a job with a creative agency near D.C., and when Sam left the military he joined her there. He'd worked as a horizontal construction engineer while he was enlisted, and once he was settled in with Jen he took a job as an assistant superintendent with a mid-sized construction company that primarily built medical facilities like doctors' offices and hospitals, as well as business offices, schools, and municipal facilities.

The firm was what people might call "old school"—for example, they were slow to acclimate to technology, and they still performed a lot of bid work. But it was a good company, and Sam felt lucky to be there. He liked how ethical the owners were and how much they cared about their employees. He excelled, and within three years he'd earned a promotion to superintendent and started taking on larger projects. He was grateful to cut his teeth with a company he respected, but after seven years he felt more than ready for whatever was next.

Sam also felt lucky to have Alan as a resource. Pleased that Sam had turned his interest in construction into a career, Alan loved to talk shop with Sam and was happy to offer guidance and answer questions wherever he could. They frequently communicated over email, and the proliferation of smart phones had made texting so convenient. Sam was eager to learn, as always, and greatly benefited from Alan's mentorship, even from over a thousand miles away.

Phone calls were not unusual but still far less frequent, and usually reserved for occasions like birthdays and Christmas, so Sam was surprised to see Alan's picture pop up on his ringing phone early one morning as he was driving to work. Alan called to let him know that Andrew had died the day before. The details were scarce; Alan only said that Andrew had been part of a rescue during a direct fire engagement with enemy forces, and that he was not the only casualty. Alan couldn't talk about it and hung up quickly.

Sam had to pull over on the side of the highway to regain his composure. His face was numb, and the reality of what he had just heard couldn't fully sink in. He was dazed, and he didn't remember the rest of his drive to work that day. He'd just seen Andrew six months prior, right around Thanksgiving, which was the last time Andrew had been home before he returned to his deployment. Sam kept thinking back to that last time, trying to remember every detail so he could hang onto them. Grasping at them was like squeezing sand. He struggled for mental snapshots: the last time he'd looked at Andrew's face, the last time he'd hugged him, the last time he'd heard his voice or his loud laugh. He'd had no idea that the last time really would be the last time for any of those things. Sam felt like an important piece of him had been cut off.

He and Jen flew home for the funeral and stayed for a week. Sam was devastated. He felt disconnected, like he was under water. The news had hit Alan and Elsie terribly hard, and Sam spent as much time with Alan as he could, feeling almost like a stand-in for Andrew. Sam was now the closest thing Alan had to a son.

Alan was often silent, but he gravitated to Sam and seemed to take comfort in his presence. In the gaps they filled with small talk, the topic of relocating to Texas came up, and Alan had offered to help him find a job with his firm, ProCon Builders, if Sam wanted. Sam couldn't think of anything he wanted more.

Andrew's premature death caused a shift with Sam and Jen. Time was passing and things at home in Texas were changing. First the loss of Sam's dad, and now Andrew, too. They felt a shared urgency to make things happen. What had always been casual, someday talk of moving back to Texas turned quickly to planning. They began shopping for a home, and eight months later they were standing next to a moving truck, with Sam brushing a tear from Jen's cheek.

"Are you ready?" Sam asked, squeezing Jen's hand.

"I can't wait," she said, smiling. "Let's go."

Chapter One

Daily Huddles

It was surprisingly chilly on Monday morning as Sam Brooks, Project Superintendent for ProCon Builders, pulled into the parking lot. His dashboard's thermostat told him it was fifty-two degrees outside, and he took a long swig of black coffee from his Thermos as he surveyed his vacant jobsite through the dusty windshield. It didn't look like much right now, but Sam felt like he already knew every inch of the facility he was building.

It was the kind of project any superintendent would be excited to have for his own: a beautifully designed three-story medical office building, totaling 75,000 square feet, located within a bustling suburb of Dallas–Fort Worth. It was Sam's first project for ProCon Builders since joining the firm nine months ago. His friend and mentor, Alan Phillips, who was a senior superintendent with ProCon, worked hard to help him get this job, and he wanted to make him proud. Sam knew this was his chance to really show everyone what he was capable of. With a wife at home and his first baby on the way, he was determined to make this project shine.

If all of that wasn't enough to keep him awake at night, this facility wasn't just any ordinary medical office building. The client was one of ProCon Builders' most important: St. Claire Health System. The build had a very strict deadline since it was the first domino to fall on six more phases of work at the main hospital, which was next door on the same campus. Everything subsequent had been planned around its timely completion.

Because the project was so prominent, Sam felt like all eyes were on him. The system's board was populated with important townspeople who held the purse strings; there had been a few articles about the new facility in the paper already; and the city's mayor had been a guest of honor at the groundbreaking. ProCon Builders' CEO, who lived four blocks away, even drove past his site twice a day on his way to and from the office.

But today, Sam was encouraged. Sure, the project's schedule was off by a few weeks, but it was early enough that Sam wasn't worried. He'd been there before, and he believed they had ample opportunity to correct course. The blistering summer was finally behind them, the building was topped out, and Sam was excited to generate new momentum with the team as they started interior partitions on the first floor.

He checked the time. The subcontractor meeting was in only thirty minutes; he still needed to review and print copies of his schedule and get the coffee brewing before the men hit the trailer. He wanted to set the tone by being prepared.

Roberto Garcia, with B&B Electric, was the first to arrive, as usual, and he'd thoughtfully picked up a couple dozen doughnuts on his way in. The other trades slowly shuffled into the trailer's cramped meeting room, and the men occupied themselves with their phones or laptops. Despite the hot coffee and sugary breakfast, Sam could tell that the mood in the room was as chilly as the temperature had been in the parking lot. To break the ice, he tried to start the meeting by asking everyone about their weekend, but no one seemed to notice. Bobby MacRae, with A+ Drywall, never looked up from his phone. Hank Hansen, the mechanical foreman for Omni Mechanical, and Jim Richards, the plumbing foreman for Infinity Plumbing, were busy picking over what was left of the doughnuts, and Tom Moretti, the foreman from Five Star Fire Suppression, was frowning at the schedule Sam had laid out on the table in front of him.

"OK, listen up, guys!" Sam announced in a voice he hoped was friendly but stern. "It's important that we hit these dates on the schedule this week. We have a great opportunity here to catch up on the schedule with the interior partitions, so we can get rough-in started on the walls. I want us to regain some of the time we lost to weather delays when we were coming out of the ground."

The group talked for over an hour and a half, but when the meeting ended Sam couldn't shake the feeling that it didn't go as well as he'd hoped. Replaying the meeting in his head, he recalled that about a third of the trades arrived late or did not attend. Guys were answering their phones in the middle of his scheduling conversations, and eyes were starting to glaze over about twenty minutes in. Sam tried to keep them engaged, but it seemed like the foremen either didn't want to speak up, or only wanted to gripe about problems without offering any solutions. On top of that, it was hard to understand where everyone was going to be working, because the subcontractors were not communicating with each other at all.

The day didn't turn out much better. Thirty minutes after the meeting, Sam's phone began to ring off the hook. He became frustrated as multiple trades called him with issues that he thought could have easily been discussed and coordinated as a team at the meeting earlier that morning. The flood of phone calls and fire drills ate up Sam's lunch hour while he went hungry, and still had him working into the evening.

Sam was defeated, and he called Alan on his ride home. Alan was ProCon Builders' "go-to guy" for all of their large, complex, and specialty projects. With thirty-two years of experience, he was a bottomless well of information. Alan was also very well respected—not just at ProCon Builders, but with other GCs in the region and with the local trades. He was the kind of guy who could take command of any room with authority but still come across as friendly and likable, and Sam admired him for that skill. Even though he was always busy, Alan still answered his phone whenever anyone needed help.

Sam told him about the subcontractor meeting and the lack of progress or urgency the trades exhibited, but before he could move on to share details from the rest of the day, Alan interrupted him.

"How often are you getting the trades in the same room to talk?"

"Once a week," Sam replied confidently.

"That's great. And how long are they talking?" asked Alan.

"Usually about an hour. Sometimes more," said Sam, still feeling good about his answers.

"Did everyone participate?" Alan quizzed.

Sam chuckled. "About as much as they always do."

"Well, what I mean is, did they talk to each other specifically about what work they'd planned for that day, what their constraints were, and exactly where they were going to be working onsite?" Alan pressed.

Now Sam thought for a moment before answering. "No, that is definitely not what's happening," he admitted.

Alan smiled. "I've had a million subcontractor meetings like that. I think I can help. How about I swing by your jobsite tomorrow morning?"

● ● ●

Alan arrived at 6:30 a.m., armed with a bag of warm breakfast tacos. Sam had gotten there thirty minutes earlier, and he was anxiously awaiting whatever their conversation would hold.

"I've got chorizo with egg, bacon with potato, and bean with cheese. What'll it be?" Alan asked.

"I'll take a chorizo and egg, thanks!" Sam replied, as he carefully opened tiny containers of salsa.

They were barely two bites into their breakfast tacos when Alan got started. "All right, Sam. Tell me what the schedule shows the team working on this week."

Sam pulled yesterday's schedule out of a pile of papers nearby and pushed it towards Alan. "I'm trying to get ahead of framing and in-wall rough-in on the first floor," he said, pointing at the line for drywalling with a greasy finger. "We have significant weather delays to recoup."

"Gotcha," replied Alan, sliding some napkins over to Sam. "How many crews are working, and for which trades?"

"Our drywall subcontractor has one framing crew, one drywall top-out crew..." Sam replied though a mouthful of chorizo and egg. He swallowed, and continued, "...and we have one crew each for electrical, mechanical, plumbing, and fire sprinkler."

"Sounds good. So, what constraints do you have on the job this week that could stop these crews from getting this work done?" asked Alan.

"Well, the guys have been complaining that we need rip rap at the construction entrances because of all the rain we've been getting. Two trucks got stuck last week, and if it rains as forecast on Thursday, it might happen again."

"Anything else?"

"Well, we've been waiting on an RFI response from the design team. We need to resolve a wall layout issue that's affecting an area we're supposed to complete this week. The architect has been sitting on the RFI for a month and the guys are frustrated."

Alan ate silently and waited.

Sam continued. "Infinity Plumbing isn't keeping up because they haven't adequately staffed their crew—and what's worse is they're still doing rework on the first floor, which is affecting the number of guys that're supposed to be working on the second floor this week." He looked out the window at his jobsite and frowned.

"Did the foremen commit to firm delivery dates at your meeting, to ensure materials would arrive as needed?" Alan inquired.

"'*Commit*'? That's a strong word," Sam quipped. "They said they would *try*."

"Did everyone leave the room on the same page for the next milestone's completion date?" Alan pressed.

"No," Sam replied quietly, examining his half-eaten breakfast taco. "I can't say that they did."

"OK. Let me ask you one last question," Alan said. "Did you guys talk about any of this at your meeting with the subcontractors yesterday?"

Sam shook his head. He felt embarrassed now, like he'd been doing something wrong. But he knew that the way he ran his work and his subcontractor meetings was typical.

Alan sensed what Sam was feeling. "Look, this is normal stuff, right? Every project, every subcontractor meeting, this is just the way it is." He took the last breakfast taco and offered it to Sam, who waved it off. "But you can run your jobs differently if you want to," Alan continued. "For example, have you thought about meeting with the trades every morning for about fifteen minutes instead of a long meeting once a week?"

Sam laughed. "I don't think we could cover one topic in fifteen minutes!"

Alan smiled. "You know what? I thought that, too, the first time someone asked me that question. But it works. For the last several years now, instead of having one long subcontractor meeting each week, like the one you had yesterday, I have a fifteen-minute meeting with the trades every morning. The time is short, so you have to be structured. The meeting starts and finishes on time," Alan said, holding up one finger. Alan was looking right at him, and Sam knew he was serious with the way he said *on time*. He picked up his pen and started taking notes.

"No one has their phones out. Everyone needs to be engaged here," he continued, now holding up two fingers. "We table issues that don't involve the entire team until after the meeting. I want to keep things moving." Sam glanced up and saw Alan holding up three fingers.

"Next, we go around the room and each foreman will tell the group *what they are working on, where they are working, how many men are in their crew,* and *what constraints are in their way,*" Alan concluded, speaking slower than usual so Sam could write down what he was saying.

At that moment the trailer door swung open, and Bobby MacRae with A+ Drywall came in for his morning coffee. Bobby was a straight shooter with a strong work ethic, who came up in the business working for his grandfather, who had owned a small, light commercial construction company for more than forty years. Under his grandpa's critical eye, Bobby had learned a diversity of trades and subsequently developed a real passion and talent for framing and drywall. After fifteen years of hard work, A+ Drywall made him their top foreman in recognition of his mentorship to their craft workers, his superior coordination of jobsite logistics, his ability to build relationships with other trade foremen and the superintendents on his projects, and his leadership in their "A+ Injury-Free Safety Program." He and Alan had once worked together on a large greenfield hospital project a few years ago; Bobby respected him and was glad to see him.

"Hey, Bobby, good to see you!" Alan said, rising to his feet. The men shook hands and took a minute to catch up. Then Alan had an idea. "Listen, help me out here for a second, would you?" he asked, gesturing towards a seat.

"Sure, what's up?" Bobby replied, settling into his chair.

"I'm walking Sam through the idea of daily huddles," said Alan. "Can you be our guinea pig?"

"Well, I can handle the pig part, anyway," Bobby laughed, patting his belly.

Sam picked up the empty taco bag and held it upside down. "Glad we got through these before you showed up, then!" he joked.

Bobby laughed and threatened to show up earlier the next day. "OK, I'm happy to help," Bobby said, nodding towards Sam. "Go ahead."

Sam quickly reviewed his notes. "Bobby, can you please tell us what you're working on, where you're working, how many men are in your crew, and what might keep you from getting your job done today?"

Suddenly, Bobby was all business. "I'm standing walls in Area B, and I have four framers and one laborer. I really need that layout RFI answer resolved so I can get it finished," he replied seriously, pressing his index finger into the table.

"OK, Bobby," Alan interjected, looking at Sam with intent. "We'll write down that constraint and get you an answer as soon as possible." Sam took the cue and wrote down the RFI constraint.

"Now," Alan coaxed, "what about your deliveries?"

"I have a load of two bundles of studs and one bundle of track coming on Thursday. It's supposed to rain again Thursday, and I'm worried about the truck getting stuck in the entrance like last week," Bobby replied.

"I hear you, Bobby," said Sam, taking control. "I'll write that down, too, and be sure to get rip rap ordered so it's resolved before your delivery."

"Do you know the upcoming milestone for the project?" Alan asked.

Bobby laughed while elbowing Sam and replied, "Yes! As per Sam's schedule, we need Area B to be framed out by next Friday. It's doable, but..." Bobby hesitated a moment, looking quickly from Alan to Sam. He decided to be honest. "But it would be nice to have some input on that next time."

"Noted!" Alan said, looking at Sam with a grin.

"Sorry about that," Sam said, smiling sheepishly. He made eye contact with Bobby and nodded his head decisively. "Next time."

As Bobby left the trailer to line out his guys, Sam turned to Alan, lowered his voice, and said, "Look, I really appreciate the help here, but I already have these kinds of conversations with the guys throughout the day."

"Oh, I know you do. But you're having them in a silo, not in a team setting," Alan replied matter-of-factly, gathering up their trash. He noticed that Sam still looked skeptical. "Do this: set up a huddle with your entire team, every day, for the rest of this week. Have this kind of conversation with each trade, with everyone in attendance. OK? Then we'll catch up over a beer next Friday afternoon and you can tell me how it went."

"Sounds like a plan," said Sam, clapping Alan on the shoulder. "Beer's on me."

●●●

Sam briefly rounded up the guys after lunch to let them know that he was going to try something different the rest of that week, and that he required their participation for a fifteen-minute daily huddle starting at 7:00 a.m. sharp each morning. The men could tell he was serious about the start time, which wasn't welcome news, and they were reluctant to add another meeting every day. However, Sam seemed intent in his belief that it would ultimately make things easier for them, so they were willing to give it a shot for a few days.

Wednesday morning arrived, and the foremen filtered into the trailer. Sam started the meeting by going over the ground rules that Alan provided the day before.

"All right, guys," Sam announced. "Here is how this works. Each of you will answer the five questions I've put on this whiteboard, and I'll keep track of your issues and the constraints that might keep work from being completed."

Roberto with B&B Electric went first. He explained that he had four electricians wrapping up wall rough-in on Area A, and that he was getting ready to move to Area B. His constraints included A+ Drywall completing their layout and wall framing so his crew could follow behind in sequence and not be shut down.

Bobby threw his hands up and said, "Roberto, I told you yesterday that I was still waiting on that stupid layout RFI. If I could get an answer on that, then we could get out of your way."

Sam eagerly jumped in. "Today is your lucky day. We ran this issue up the pole with the design team, and they said we'll have the detail after lunch. Can you commit to Roberto that you will be ahead of him for his wall rough?"

Bobby looked relieved. "If I have the answered RFI, then yeah, I can commit!"

Roberto finished up by telling the team that he did not have any deliveries scheduled for the week, and that he understood the upcoming milestone, which he determined was "tight but feasible." The rest of the foremen followed suit, until all subcontractors had a turn. As the guys disbanded and went back into the field, Sam looked at his watch and saw that the huddle took around thirty minutes. While he was disappointed that it went so long, he couldn't believe the amount of buy-in and problem solving that occurred between the trades.

By the second week he realized that, even though he had worked with these guys for all of this time, he did not really know much about them and their personal lives. Sam decided to start each huddle with quick icebreakers like the "stranded on the beach" question, or "two truths and a lie," and sharing fun or weird facts about themselves. As it turned out, the trade foremen had more in common with each other than they thought. For example, Jim's son played football at the same high school as Bobby's daughter, who was on the softball team, and they knew a handful of the same people. As the week went on, the foremen started to become more comfortable sharing things with one another about their work activities, needs, and constraints. By the following week, Sam started to notice small but encouraging improvements in the project's overall workflow reliability. He couldn't wait to tell Alan all about it.

Sam pulled up to the Smoke Pit at 4:00 p.m. on Friday after a very productive week. Alan was waiting at the bar with two cold draughts as Sam walked in. The men greeted each other and then moved to two stools away from the crowd where they could talk more easily.

"So, what's going on this weekend?" Alan asked. "Anything fun?"

"Well, I thought I was going to have to work all weekend, but the guys really turned it around after our first huddle. Now I think we'll only need to put in a half-day on Saturday," Sam answered. "Looks like I'll get to watch the game Sunday! So, *I'm* happy, but I can't speak for my wife," he joked.

Alan laughed. "That's great! How'd you get there?"

"Remember that RFI that Bobby mentioned, that was holding up his framing on Area A?" Sam asked, and Alan affirmed with a nod. "We had a conference call with the design team and let them know what impact this was having on the schedule. They felt accountable for holding up the team, and they got it to us the next day. Resolving the RFI allowed A+ to commit to B&B that they would complete the wall framing that was stalling the electrical rough."

"That's fast," Alan said, smiling. "Good job."

Sam took a long pull on his beer. "We really dodged a bullet on Thursday with the storms just north of the jobsite, but I made a commitment to the team to get the rip rap in and I was able to have it installed Wednesday afternoon. The guys appreciated that."

"Awesome," said Alan. "Feels good to know someone has your back, right?"

"Right," Sam agreed. "And today was our most productive day all week, because the team was able to collaborate and work through a coordination issue with material staging at our morning huddle. It looked like a major obstacle for installing wall rough on schedule, but the team talked through it and found a solution that seems like it will work for everyone."

"This kind of stuff is so good to hear," Alan said, sincerely pleased.

"Listen, I really appreciate the tip on the daily huddles. I didn't think it would make a big difference, but I can see the impact that it's having on the team," Sam confessed.

"Glad to help," Alan smiled and clinked Sam's mug with his own. "Sounds like you are off to a great start in shaking up the way you run work."

"'*A start*'?" Sam mused, wide-eyed.

Alan laughed. "Yes, it's a start. There's more you can do—a lot more, if you're interested. Let's talk again after the superintendent safety stand-down."

Chapter Two

Visual Communication

Alan had just finished his safety presentation on fall protection at the superintendent safety stand-down. As the other ProCon Builders superintendents said their good-byes and drifted towards the parking lot, Sam helped Alan finish bagging the trash and wiping down the tables in the trailer. Alan noticed his friend seemed distracted. The last time he'd seen Sam, he was upbeat and happy about the progress on his job. That seemed to be over.

"So, how's it going this week?"

"Oh, you know, it's fine," replied Sam, trying to sound more confident than he felt. He didn't want to admit to Alan that the success he'd had with the huddles over the last few weeks hadn't lasted. Sam finished cleaning off the table, but Alan seemed to be waiting for him to continue talking. "It's just that we are still struggling with daily communication," Sam admitted.

"Give me some examples."

"Well," Sam began hesitantly, "Monday's daily huddle was bumpy. Tuesday's huddle wasn't much better. The huddle meetings have been getting longer each day. Jim, the foreman with Infinity Plumbing spent eight minutes soapboxing about a late plumbing fixture submittal for fixtures that aren't even due on-site for several weeks, and that really don't affect any of the other trades."

Alan nodded and waited for Sam to go on.

"I've also noticed that the trades don't really pay attention when the other trades are talking about where they are working."

Alan smirked. "What? That never happens!"

Sam smiled, and then continued. "It's a real problem, though. A specific instance came up in the field, when Bobby with A+ Drywall misunderstood where Roberto with B&B Electric was trying to get their partial in-wall inspections. This led to A+ covering up 2,000 square feet of wall, a failed inspection, and rework. Roberto was furious, and things got very tense." Too familiar with Roberto's temper, Alan winced.

Roberto Garcia came from a family that built things, but the two men who had the most influence over him were his father, a carpenter, and his uncle, an electrician. Starting at a young age, Roberto helped on various projects and in his dad's workshop, where he learned valuable skills in both trades. While he was very bright and learned easily, patience was not among his virtues, and he dropped out of high school to begin his career as a carpenter when he was only sixteen. He switched gears at eighteen to work for his uncle, who clearly saw Roberto's potential and urged him to apply for his apprentice license. Four years later, he received his journeyman's license, and he subsequently took a job with B&B Electric to grow into larger work. Within a few years, he sat for his exam and became the youngest Master Electrician B&B had ever employed.

Alan had worked with Roberto on a surgery center project in the past and knew his attention to detail and safety to be impeccable. However, Alan also knew him to be temperamental, stubborn, and sometimes difficult to work with—qualities he chalked up to Roberto's youth more than a failing of his character.

Sam noticed Alan's expression and nodded. "Roberto was *hot*. And so were Bobby's tape-and-bed crew, who had started pre-bedding close to half of the walls that were rocked."

"Well, that's a real trainwreck," Alan concluded.

Sam looked sad. "I have to do most of the talking. Once the guys take a seat, the phones come out and some guys even start falling asleep. Yesterday, I was fed up and got short with the foremen. It's like they're too used to being told where they should be working and what they're supposed to be working on. They act like they don't know how to speak up for themselves."

They were quiet for a moment. Alan watched Sam's face for a hint of what might be going through his mind. "Thinking about going back to the old way?" Alan asked with a grin.

"No way!" Sam exclaimed. "Even with these issues, it's still an improvement from the way I did it before. I'm just frustrated."

Alan understood Sam's feelings all too well. He nodded and said, "Tell you what, how about I swing by your site again tomorrow afternoon to share a few more things that I think could help?"

Sam smiled and nodded.

"Great," said Alan, grabbing his keys. "I'll see you then."

Alan arrived at the jobsite around 4:30 p.m. After shooting the breeze with Sam about Monday night's Cowboys game, Alan started folding up the metal chairs and placing them in the next room.

"Hang on, Alan—I need those out here for tomorrow morning's huddle."

Alan folded the chair he'd just picked up and tucked it around the corner. "This is a *huddle*, right? When was the last time you saw the Cowboys sit for a pre-play huddle?"

"Huh, I hadn't thought of it that way," Sam replied, folding a chair of his own. "Makes sense."

Alan smiled and handed Sam the last chair. "I still have a few tricks up my sleeve, and one is in the bed of my truck. Come give me a hand."

As Alan dropped the tailgate, Sam took a quick inventory and then gave Alan a puzzled look. "Plastic laminate, and a brown bag filled with..." Sam rifled through the bag. "...an egg timer, a stuffed teddy bear wearing a red bow tie, and dry erase markers?"

"You'll see," said Alan, who was enjoying Sam's confusion.

As they walked back to the trailer, Alan asked for Sam's latest floor plan, a drill, and some screws.

"OK," Alan said, surveying the items they'd assembled. "If I remember correctly, the first issue you described was that the meetings were taking too long. Here's how I've resolved that." Alan reached into the brown paper sack and tossed the egg timer to Sam.

"Set this for fifteen minutes, and when it goes off the meeting is finished, no matter what. The guys will get used to only talking about the important stuff."

Sam turned the egg timer over in his hand. "OK, I like it, but what about when a guy goes on a filibuster?"

"That's when this little dude comes in." Alan reached into the sack and pulled out the teddy bear. "Do you know who this is?"

"What are you doing with a toy?" Sam asked incredulously.

"He's not a toy! He's a mean old bear named 'Elmo,' and E.L.M.O. is an acronym, Sam. It stands for 'Enough, let's move on.' Next time someone goes off script, throw this guy at him and call 'Elmo!' Let him know that what he has to say is important, but it's not information the entire team needs to hear, so it's going into the 'parking lot' for after the meeting. The 'parking lot' is where we capture items that are important but aren't relevant at the huddle. These are discussed later, and only with the right people, so we don't waste time and get the others off track."

"Got it," Sam affirmed. "What about this?" He nudged the laminate with his boot.

Alan scanned the room. "This goes...there." He pointed at the far wall, opposite the door.

Sam and Alan cleared the space and hung the laminate with long screws. Alan began placing the floor plans behind the laminate.

As he worked, he asked Sam to make a key with each dry erase marker color to represent the different subcontractors that Sam currently had in the field.

"Can you remind me of that issue that you had earlier in the week that caused rework between the electrician and the drywall trades?" Alan asked.

Sam groaned. "Roberto, with B&B Electric, was explaining that he had spoken to the electrical inspector and that he was good to go with a partial inspection to cover up walls in Area A. Problem was, he forgot to mention he was only talking about Area A on the *first floor*, not the *second floor*. Bobby with A+ Drywall started in Area A on the second floor and darn near had it all rocked out before Roberto's guys realized what was going on. Those two screamed at each other for five minutes, with Roberto swearing up and down that he told Bobby the correct floor."

Alan nodded as he reviewed the floor plans "I wish I could say this hasn't happened to me before. So, here's something I do that helps to keep it from happening to me *again*." He picked up a dry erase marker and handed it to Sam. "At your next huddle, ask each trade foreman to come up to the board and indicate what his activity is, where he is working, how many people he'll have for the activity, and what is in his way. This will force the team to collaborate at a higher level and can help everyone avoid those types of miscommunications."

Sam studied the wall and was able to imagine exactly what Alan was describing. He liked it.

"I'm willing to bet you a steak dinner and a cold beer that you'll begin to see your workflow become much more reliable in the field if you give this a shot," Alan added.

Sam was impressed. He couldn't believe he'd never seen anyone doing this before. "This just makes so much sense!" he blurted.

Alan laughed and put his arm around Sam's shoulder. "Listen, my friend, this sounds easy, but don't get discouraged if it takes a few days, or even a week or two for the guys to go along with you on this. It'll put a few of them outside their comfort zone, having to go up to the board and tell everyone about what they're doing and where they're doing it. But it'll be worth the extra effort you put into making this work."

"I really appreciate all the help," said Sam, who had started to look forward to his Friday morning huddle. "I'll check in with you in a few weeks and let you know how this goes."

"Sounds good," Alan said. He picked up Elmo the bear and shoved it at Sam. "Let's get out of here."

● ● ●

Over the next few days, as Alan had predicted, there were some rough patches with the morning huddles. It took a little time for the guys to get used to not having chairs and, when the timer went off, they were only halfway through the topics they were used to talking about. But by the following Monday, the trade foremen were getting used to their new rhythm. After they arrived in the trailer, they picked up their markers and went straight to the floor plan boards, ready to get down to business.

Hank, with Omni Mechanical, was the first to start. "OK, guys, I have two crews of four tin benders installing main trunk lines and branch lines in Area B on the first floor," he explained, as he carefully drew a cloud-shaped circle on the plans with his orange marker to indicate his planned work area for the day.

"Great!" Sam encouraged. "Is there anything in your way that might stop you from getting that done today?" Hank shook his head to indicate that he didn't anticipate any issues. "Good deal," Sam replied. "Who's next?"

"I'll go," volunteered Bobby from A+ Drywall. "OK, I'm going to have multiple crews of three, and they're working in these three areas," Bobby explained as he drew big blue clouds with his marker signifying the three different locations where his men would be installing framing and topping out walls. "As far as I can see, nothing is in our way today, Sam," he added, snapping the cap back on his dry erase marker.

Sam was loving this. "Sounds great! Thank you. All right, Jim, you're up."

Jim, from Infinity Plumbing, approached the board and used his green marker to slowly circle the locations where his plumbers were working. "Sam, I'm going to be honest with you, I've got some issues today!" Jim exclaimed, taking Sam by surprise. "We're trying to finish our commitment of roughing-in walls in Area A so we can get that partial cover-up inspection by Friday, but my supply house is screwing me up right now. They still can't get the pro-press copper elbows I need to finish roughing-in the bathrooms!"

"ALL of the bathrooms?" asked Bobby, who was thinking about the impact of this on his anticipated workload for the following week.

"No, just the second floor," answered Jim. "They shorted us! Let me tell you something, I've been a loyal customer with Johnston Supply for over twenty years. George Johnston, who I have known forever—I mean, he went to high school with my dad, you know? They were in the class of sixty-eight together. Go Skeeters! Anyway, he founded Johnston Supply back in the seventies, but he retired and sold out a few years back. These new people, man, it's just not the same! George was a good guy, see, he had his act together, and he wouldn't have ever shorted me on an order this way. But these new owners—OK, so, my last project was a two-story dormitory expansion for Sandhill College..."

At that moment, Elmo the bear sailed across the room and smacked Jim in the chest, freezing him in his tracks. "No one cares about the stupid Skeeters or your stupid dormitory project, Jim!" Roberto shouted.

"It's Skeeter Story Time, kids!" Tom laughed. Another subcontractor called out, "We need milk and cookies!" There was more laughter from the group as Jim picked up Elmo and bounced him off Tom's hard hat.

Sam smiled. "Jim, what you're saying is important, but it's just too much information and it's not relevant to everyone at the huddle. But I wrote your issue down in the 'parking lot' on my notepad, and we'll regroup after the huddle to see what we can do to expedite your shorted material, OK? Is there anything else you need to bring up right now?" Jim shook his head no and gave Sam a thumbs up.

The meeting continued with the rest of the trades illustrating where their men were working and letting everyone know about the constraints they had, if any. The last foreman was wrapping up when...*DING!*

The men stopped and looked at the egg timer. "OK, that's our fifteen minutes!" Sam announced. "Anyone with 'parking lot' items, please stay behind. Jim, call Johnston Supply and let's see what's the latest."

The foremen began to maneuver down the wobbly aluminum stairs and towards the jobsite. As they walked, Tom put his arm around Roberto and said, "Nice shot with Elmo, my friend! You saved us!"

Roberto laughed and replied, "I'm not going to lie, I was skeptical about this whole 'huddle, visual boards, new tools' thing Sam's been pushing on us, but I have to admit things seem to be running smoother here than on my last few jobs."

Tom paused for a moment and then agreed. "Come to think of it—mine, too."

The visual communication tools were really put to the test late the next week. Roberto was walking his afternoon job rounds and stumbled upon Hank, who was at work installing his main supply trunk lines coming out of the riser shaft on the first floor.

"HANK! What the heck are you doing?" Roberto barked.

"What the heck does it *look* like I'm doing, Roberto?" Hank snapped back. "I'm running duct! We got ahead in Area B, and I decided to keep the guys moving and jump ahead in Area C."

Sam happened to be walking down the corridor at that moment, and he overheard the guys arguing. He stopped to listen.

"You are running your gigantic ductwork right where I'm scheduled to run my homerun conduit bank on Thursday?!" Roberto shrieked. "I was very clear in this morning's huddle. I told the team that this is where my crews were moving tomorrow. I filled in the floor plan with my color and put the date I would be in this area!" Roberto knew he had been doing his best to go along with Sam's huddles, and he felt betrayed by what he saw as Hank's thoughtless intrusion.

Hank had come down from his ladder with every intention of arguing back, but as he listened to Roberto he realized his error.

"Man, Roberto, you're right!" Hank said. "I remember now, you did mark up the board."

Roberto was too surprised to respond.

"I was just trying to get ahead since we finished Area B a day early. I didn't realize this was going to impact your workflow. I'll pull this piece of ductwork down and reschedule once you're done with your homerun conduit bank."

Roberto studied the duct for a moment and then responded, "You know what, Hank, you can leave that one up. I'll have my guys work around that one piece. Just don't put any more up."

Hank smiled. "Hey, I appreciate that."

"No problem," said Roberto. "Sorry I got hot."

Sam was elated. He couldn't remember the last time an issue was resolved in the field without his involvement and having to weigh in—especially when Roberto was involved.

Over the next couple of weeks, the team was finishing the daily huddles in fifteen minutes, and the guys were doing a great job marking up the boards with their dry erase markers in the mornings. They were starting to break out into smaller groups at the end of the huddles to work through logistics without needing Sam's direction. Some were even voluntarily circling back at the end of the day, before their crews left, to make sure they'd followed through on the day's commitments. As Sam locked up the jobsite on Friday afternoon, he felt encouraged about the momentum the team was generating in leveraging these new tools.

Things weren't perfect, however. He still hadn't figured out how to recover the lost time on the overall project schedule, and the thought made Sam feel a little sick with anxiety.

Chapter Three

The Eight Wastes

It was 11:00 a.m. on a Monday, and Sam was weighing the pros and cons of three kinds of wood screws at Builder's Warehouse. Heavy winds over the weekend had damaged a large section of the site fence, and he was using his lunch hour to stock up on materials they'd need to make the repairs. He'd just finished a hot dog he'd picked up from the stand in front of the store when his phone buzzed in his back pocket. It was Hank with Omni Mechanical.

While Sam liked and respected all of the men he worked with, he probably had the easiest rapport with Hank Hansen. Both men were veterans, and Hank, a former staff sergeant with the Marines, loved to jokingly poke Sam about the Corps' superiority to all other branches of the military—taking as evidence anything he could find, however small or irrelevant.

Hank learned to weld in the Marines, where he was a metal worker responsible for repairing a diversity of tools, equipment, and vehicles. After his discharge, he joined Omni Mechanical and worked in their fabrication shop. Because of his strong leadership skills he was moved to the field, where he'd quickly worked his way up to foreman.

"Hey, Hank! What's up?"

"Well, I've got good news and bad news. Which do you want first?"

Sam frowned at the box of two-inch wood screws in his hand. "OK. Hit me with the bad."

"About twenty feet of fence is lying down on the northeast part of the site," replied Hank. "Looks like the wind got it pretty good."

"Yeah, I saw that. But I heard that an Omni truck backed into it," Sam joked.

"THAT'S A LIE!" Hank shouted with mock outrage. "We were going FORWARD when we ran over it."

Sam laughed. "That's how they teach you guys to drive in the Corps?"

"I think that truck driver served with the coast guard, actually." Hank retorted. "OK, so the good news is I just got off the phone with my shop foreman, and this middle school project we have going in Arlington got pushed back a few weeks. We're able to bump up all of the ductwork for the second floor in the production line. We can deliver all of it onsite this Wednesday if that's OK with you?"

Sam was overjoyed. "I think that's the best news I've heard all day!" he exclaimed. "That should really help with our overhead production on the second floor and speed things up. Let's do it!"

Sam called his project manager, Gene Hudson, as he drove back to the jobsite. Gene was only a few years older than Sam, but he'd spent his entire career at a much larger firm in Oklahoma before he had moved to Texas and joined ProCon Builders three years earlier. One of a handful of "Okies" at ProCon, Gene loved to indulge in the Texas/OU rivalry and goad his coworkers, and his annual "Red River Showdown" parties were already legendary. Gene's experience on larger and more complex projects had proven to be a real asset, and Sam was really enjoying this first project with him—in fact, they had gotten along so well, Gene had invited Sam to go dove hunting this coming fall with him in western Oklahoma, where he and his brothers owned a few dozen acres.

Sam relayed all of the details from Hank's call, and Gene felt as encouraged as Sam did that this might be the turning point in their schedule to get things back on track.

"I'll update the Gantt with this new info and see what it does for us," Gene said. "Let's hope it shaves off a week or more."

"Excellent, thanks! Let me know what you see."

Four truckloads of ductwork began to arrive as planned at 7:30 a.m. on Wednesday, right after the morning huddle. Hank instructed his crews to stage it in each area where it would be installed, and Sam looked out over the second floor and all the neatly stacked duct with a satisfied smile. He couldn't believe his good fortune with the early delivery of so much material; he knew this was going to have a great impact on his schedule. He was walking back to the trailer when his phone rang.

"Alan!" Sam was happy to hear from him, since it had been a few weeks since they last spoke. "How's it going in Fort Worth?"

"Hey Sam, everything's good! We're tracking three weeks early for the final inspection on the last area of the bed tower. The client is chomping at the bit to open beds, so they're happy."

"That's awesome! Congrats, man."

"Thank you! It was tough, but we pulled it off. I want to catch up on your job, too, but first I'm checking in with all the superintendents to make sure everyone saw and understood the new equipment rental agreements that corporate sent last week."

"Yep, I got that. It makes sense to me," Sam affirmed.

"Roger that," Alan concluded. "So, fill me in on the MOB?"

"Things are humming here," Sam replied gratefully. "The visual communication tools you helped me with have made a big impact on our productivity and the reliability of the work in the field. I can't believe how well the foremen have adapted to the changes."

"I'm glad to hear it! Look, I am about to step into an owner meeting, but I'm making a trip to the main office next week. Want to have lunch and fill me in on the details?"

Sam pulled up his calendar. "How's Tuesday?"

"That works." Alan affirmed. "Tuesday it is."

"Wait!" Sam interjected. "I have a better idea—how about you come to our morning huddle? You can walk the job with me, and then we can head to that great barbecue joint over on Pearson that I've told you about."

"I'd like that," Alan answered, sincerely pleased. "I appreciate you inviting me to walk your job with you."

"Hey, I'm always happy to have you visit," Sam replied with a smile. "I'll see you then."

It was 6:45 a.m., and Sam had just put on a fresh pot of coffee as the trades entered the trailer. He and Alan had arrived early and spent some time together reviewing the schedule. Now Alan was eating a sausage biscuit while catching up with a few of the guys. At 7:00 a.m. sharp, Sam set the timer and started the huddle. Bobby, with A+ Drywall, went first, and he used his blue dry erase marker to draw X's to indicate his team's activity over three areas.

"The schedule indicates that this is where we're supposed to be hanging drywall this week." Bobby announced to the room. "Instead, I am completely shut down."

Sam was caught off guard. "Wait...*what?* What do you mean?"

"There are huge stacks of ductwork all over the place on the second floor!" snapped Tom from Five Star Fire Suppression. He walked up to the board with his red marker and drew X's in three other locations. "My guys are also shut down in these locations due to all the ductwork that Hank's staged up there. We can't even get our lifts in the area without running into it, which already happened once."

"ONCE?!" Hank spluttered. "Your guys are having a demolition derby up there with those lifts! We've had SEVERAL pieces of damaged ductwork that will need to go back to the fab shop to be reworked! I've got the boys loading them up now, and I'll be preparing a back charge for you."

"I want to know who had the bright idea to have all the duct delivered to the second floor without bringing it up in the huddle to discuss with the entire team?" Tom pressed.

Bobby turned to face Sam. "This is a real problem. Per YOUR schedule, I need the walls rocked out in Area B by next Friday, and I can tell you right now that we will have to wait until at least Thursday before we can begin rocking again. Chances of us hitting that milestone are slim at best."

Sam was mortified. This was not what he expected.

After what felt like an eternity, the timer finally signaled an end to the disastrous huddle and the men went to work. Sam took a deep breath and exhaled. "So. That went well."

Alan smiled. "Ah, keep your head up. You can learn a lot from meetings like this."

Unconvinced, Sam shook his head.

Alan was unfazed. "It sounds like you've got a pretty good issue on the second floor. Let's suit up and check it out."

As Sam and Alan were walking up the stairs to the second floor, Alan turned to Sam and asked. "Hey, Sam, have you ever heard of the 'Eight Deadly Wastes' on a jobsite?"

Sam stopped walking and thought for a moment. He felt like he should know the answer, but he didn't. "Does this have something to do with asbestos?"

Alan chuckled. "No, but good try! Have you ever heard someone use the acronym D.O.W.N.T.I.M.E.?"

He was sure he hadn't. "No. What's that?"

"The word 'downtime' helps you remember the 'Eight Wastes'. It goes like this. The first one is D for *Defects*, which has to do with materials that have been damaged or made incorrectly. These materials will have to be reworked or scrapped, and that's waste. Waste is anything that doesn't add value—or, to put it this way, waste only ADDS time and cost to your project. Make sense?" Alan asked.

"Yes," said Sam, who had begun to write this down in his notepad.

"The second waste starts with O, which represents *Overproduction*," Alan continued. "Overproduction is building something too soon, having too much of something already built, or building something quicker than is needed." As Sam was writing, he began to think back to Hank's call last week about the ductwork for the second floor, and grimaced.

Alan leaned against the wall and propped one foot on the stairs. "The third waste starts with W and looks like this," Alan said, gesturing towards himself with both thumbs.

Sam looked up at him. "Waiting?"

Alan nodded. "Yep. *Waiting* is pretty straightforward, right? Any time that work is not able to be done because of the impacts from any of the other wastes, you'll experience waiting."

Sam nodded and kept writing.

"Fourth—and my personal pet peeve—is the N, which represents *Non-Utilized Talent*." Alan said, shaking his head. "Any time a tradesman has to address one of the Eight Wastes instead of focusing on their skilled craft, they are being pulled away from their true potential and the role that brings the most value to the project.

"Fifth on the list is T, the *Transportation* waste. This is the unnecessary movement of materials. The time it takes for materials to be transported from one location to another is considered waste—and on top of that, it becomes more likely for those materials to be damaged, taking us back to where we started, with defects."

Alan nudged Sam and pointed out the window. Hank's guys were beginning to load up a bundle of the damaged ductwork.

"The sixth waste is I, for *Inventory*," Alan continued. "Having inventory may not seem like a bad thing at first, but having too much of something on a jobsite can be extremely detrimental to the flow of work. It's also a lot of money sitting on your job that could 'walk away,' if you know what I mean. And it increases the likelihood that it will need to be moved or can end up being damaged, starting the Eight Wastes cycle over again."

Sam flipped the page in his notebook, and Alan went on. "M, for *Motion*, is the seventh deadly waste. Motion involves movement by craftsman. Even what seems like a small, non-value-added motion can cost your project. For example, Sam, you've done a great job conveniently placing your port-o-johns so the guys can access them near the building. Now, imagine if you placed them on the opposite side of the parking lot. How much wasted motion would that create for the guys who'd have to go back and forth throughout the day, just to take a leak?

"And, finally, we have E. *Excess* is the eighth waste. You should think of excess as over-processing something. Anytime you need to rework, rebuild, or redesign, you are experiencing excess processing, which adds no value and only contributes to the other wastes. Excess processing can stem from lots of different situations."

Alan waited for Sam to finish his notes before he spoke again. "It's important that you recognize all of the Eight Deadly Wastes on a jobsite; otherwise, you can have serious issues when it comes to your schedule. Remember them with the D.O.W.N.T.I.M.E. acronym—Defects, Overproduction, Waiting, Non-Utilized Talent, Transportation, Inventory, Motion, and Excess."

Sam's mind was blown, and he was thankful for the benefit of Alan's experience. He tucked his pad back in his pocket and smiled. "This is really good, Alan, thank you. I'll practice watching for these."

"We can start practicing now! Let's get to the second floor and see if we identify any of the Eight Wastes. We can try to address them head on." They started back up the stairs, and after a moment, Alan asked, "Hey, what was the name of your foreman who delivered all this ductwork?"

"Hank Hansen, with Omni Mechanical. He's a good guy; he called me last week when there was an opening in his shop, and I agreed that it would be a good idea." Sam paused thoughtfully for a moment and added, "Obviously, neither of us realized the can of worms we were about to open."

"It's an understandable assumption, and we've all done it," Alan reassured him. "Can you do me a favor and see if Hank is available to walk with us?"

Hank met with them in Area B on the second floor. After Sam made the introductions, the three of them began to walk down the corridor.

"Hank, I was just explaining the 'Eight Deadly Wastes' on jobsites to Sam, and I hoped you'd walk with us as we try to identify if any are on this site," Alan explained. Hank agreed, unsure of what Alan was describing, but the word "deadly" certainly had him intrigued.

"OK," Alan began. "The first waste I see is all this ductwork stacked throughout the second floor. Sam, of the Eight Wastes, which one do you think is the root cause to the ductwork issue we have on the second floor?"

Sam pulled out his pad, referred to his notes, and thought for a moment. "I guess it all started with *Overproduction*. When Hank called me last week and said he could get a jump on running the second-floor areas in their fab shop, I thought we'd gain time. I was sure that we'd be *more productive* if we had the ductwork onsite, ready to go when we needed it."

"Yeah," Hank agreed. "I hate it when the material isn't here when we need it, so I thought it would be good to have it all delivered as soon as we could get it."

As they all gazed at the stacks of ductwork spread throughout each area, it was painfully obvious that more material onsite did not equate to more work in place. "You're right, Sam. What we're looking at is a classic case of overproduction." Alan concluded. "And Sam, what does overproduction often produce?"

Sam checked his notepad. "*Inventory.*"

"Bingo!" Alan affirmed. "That's what we are looking at, isn't it? Inventory—and lots of it."

"All over the place," Sam agreed, quietly.

But Hank was less sure. "Hold on a minute—I need this stuff," he challenged. "When it comes time to install this duct, it does me no good if it's not onsite!"

"That's true," Alan began, as he pulled a printout of the schedule from his pocket. "But do you really need all of it onsite *at the same time* if you can only install a small amount of it in one week? Take a look here," Alan continued, as they entered Area B. "According to this schedule, you don't have anyone planned for work in this area until *next week,* and no one is lined up to be in Area C for *two more weeks.* Meanwhile, all of this inventory is just sitting here, stopping Tom and Bobby from installing fire sprinkler pipe and drywall—which is work that's scheduled for *this week,* right?"

Sam nodded. "Yes, that's correct."

Hank looked at the schedule and then surveyed the room again. "I see your point," he admitted.

"So, Sam, if Tom's and Bobby's crews are not able to work, then what are they doing?"

"*Waiting!*" Sam confirmed. "That's waste number three."

"Right! But look there—not everyone is waiting." Alan pointed to a crew, busily loading ductwork onto a pallet jack on the other side of the room. "What are those guys doing over there?"

"Those are my guys, and they're moving ductwork out of the way so Bobby can complete his drywalling in Area A," defended Hank.

"Are we watching a value-added task for your guys? Meaning, is that how you make your money?" Alan quizzed.

"Noooo," Hank said, with a chuckle. "We make our money by *installing* ductwork, not by *moving it* from one place to another."

Sam didn't even need to look at his notes. "This is wasted *Motion*, Hank. And it's number six from the 'Eight Deadly Wastes.'"

Hank took Sam's pad and reviewed what he'd written down. It was starting to click into place for him, but it was now obvious to Sam: having this ductwork onsite was well-intentioned, but ultimately a very bad idea.

But Alan wasn't finished with them yet. He'd just spotted a damaged door frame leading into a room full of stored ductwork. He met eyes with Hank, and asked, "Anyone want to guess how this door frame got dinged? Or how about that twelve-inch spiral duct over in the corner? It looks pretty banged up."

Hank turned to Sam and back to Alan. "Well, *CRAP!*" was all he could muster.

"*Defects!*" Sam blurted miserably. "This stuff is going to cost me time and money."

Alan nodded as he walked to the window and looked out. "So, what is going to happen to all of this damaged ductwork?"

Sam and Hank joined Alan at the window, and together they watched Omni Mechanical's crew loading the flatbed truck.

Hank held up his hand to stop them and said, "Wait, I've got this one." He looked at Sam's notepad. "This material has to be sent back to the shop to be fixed or scrapped...and that's number five, *Transportation*," he announced.

"Unnecessary movement of materials," Sam concurred. "What a waste of time, effort, and money."

"All right," said Alan. "I think we only have two more left. Hank, when that material gets back to the shop, what's going to happen next?"

"I've already heard from the fab shop foreman. Remember that middle school project that had been delayed? Well, now he's got the green light on that, and he chewed me out about all this ductwork coming back to be reworked. He's really angry—he says he can't even begin to re-work it without pulling overtime this weekend."

"That's justified anger," acknowledged Alan. He turned to Sam and asked, "What do we call this, based on our conversation?"

"*Excess*," said Sam, who felt sick to his stomach thinking about Hank's angry fab shop foreman. "The re-working of this ductwork and the door frame are both examples of excess processing, which adds no value whatsoever."

"Which leads us to our final and most important of the Eight Deadly Wastes: *Non-Utilized Talent*. Hank, your guys, who should be *installing* ductwork in Area A, are instead spending their entire day *moving* ductwork to B and C."

Now Hank was mad at himself. "And Bobby's guys, who were supposed to be installing drywall in Area B, are now going to have to replace or repair the door frames that were damaged by moving the ductwork around."

"I'm sure I'll see a ticket for that," Sam added, sadly.

"The delivery guys, who *should be* taking material to the middle school, now have to come back here to pick up damaged ductwork, and then bring it back later when it's been repaired or remade."

"Hank, now I'm worrying about our third-floor duct. Will the same fabricators, who have to spend time repairing the ductwork from the second floor, be making new ductwork for the third floor?" Sam queried.

Hank frowned and nodded his head.

"All that wasted talent. What a shame," interjected Alan, who had been listening quietly. "When you don't feel productive, and you're spending your time on things that aren't your passion or skill, it can be really deflating and have a negative impact on your work and home life."

"I've never thought of it like that," said Sam. "But on days where it feels like we got nothing done, it does have a negative impact, and I do take it home with me."

"Same here," agreed Hank, flatly.

Sam felt defeated. "My schedule is shot! And I felt so confident this morning. I was really looking forward to showing Alan all the progress we'd made, and how the visual tools were really working."

"Look, guys, I'm not trying to make you two feel bad about this stuff with the ductwork. Our business is a journey, right? We all have successes, and we all have screw ups. We learn from our mistakes and come back the next day to do it a little better. So that's what you'll do. You'll turn this around."

"Alan, that stuff about the Eight Wastes is a lot of good food for thought," said Hank. "Thanks for bringing me in on that walk-through. Sam, I want to make a copy of your notes and share them with my guys, if that's OK?"

"Absolutely, I'm happy to."

"Sam, I think you promised me some barbecue! Join us, Hank—and let's see if Gene, Tom, and Bobby can come, too. If we put our heads together, maybe we can figure out how to minimize the schedule impacts on the second floor."

"Good idea," Sam agreed. As he pulled out his phone to start calling the guys, he was already feeling much better.

●●●

"Would you just look at this guy—he's *beautiful!*" Gene exclaimed. His face was animated as he scrolled through pictures on his smart phone, panning it back and forth across the table so Sam, Alan, Hank, Tom, and Bobby could see. "He's a 160-class buck! Check it out!" he said, zooming in closer on the deer's head. A whitetail buck had been captured on the feeder camera at his lease, and Gene was going to be up there the following week with his three brothers.

Bobby whistled with admiration as he squinted at the grainy picture. "If you nab him, I'm gonna need some jerky!"

"We'll be lucky to ever lay eyes on *this one* in person," said Gene. "But I'm pretty sure some jerky is doable!"

Sam's stomach growled, and he was glad to see the waitress appear at that moment, weighed down with a heavy tray of food. As the guys started to eat their lunch, Sam pulled out a folded copy of the second floor's floor plan and spread it out in the center of their table. He asked Bobby and Tom to draw X's on the locations where they'd indicated that they were shut down. The group quietly studied the floor plan for a couple of minutes, and then Hank broke the silence.

"Well, I can talk to my office about putting together a ticket to work tens the rest of the week, and then run two crews on Saturday. That would still put Tom and Hank behind about five days, but we would have the duct up and out of the way," Hank said with a shrug.

"Wow, *a whole week?*" Sam sighed. "I don't like the sound of that."

Gene didn't like the sound of that, either. "I'm not sure we have overtime in the budget, Hank. What else?"

Hank chewed on a rib while he thought. "Maybe we could move to nights the rest of the week? We wouldn't be completely out of the way, but there should be enough off the floor that Bobby and Tom could finish what they need to before it's time for our next night shift."

"Is there cost associated with that?" Gene asked, nervously.

"Yeah, that would be time-and-a-half for our night guys."

"We would also have to bring in a night foreman," Sam interjected. "I'm not sure I want work going on while I'm not there."

Hank felt a little irritated, and completely out of ideas. "I'm not sure we have any other options."

Bobby had an idea. He held up his hand as he swallowed his bite of brisket, and then offered his solution. "Hey guys, I think we have a large CONEX not being used on our hotel project up the street. I'll make a couple of calls—maybe I can get it dropped off first thing tomorrow. We can rally the other tradesmen and help Hank's crew get the ductwork stored in the CONEX and out of our way."

Sam thought for a moment and then looked at Alan. "Jeez, there would be *Waiting*, and *Non-Utilized Talent*, and *Transportation* and *Motion* waste with that, Bobby. I don't know."

Alan felt proud that Sam already had the types of wastes memorized, but he also knew a good idea when he heard one. "I get what you're saying, Sam, but this is a real pickle. I think the CONEX may be your best bet." Alan turned to look at Gene, and added, "If you can pull it off, it would only put you a day-and-a-half behind schedule and keep you from working overtime."

Gene met Sam's gaze and nodded. Sam turned to Bobby and confirmed, "This sounds like a winner—let's do it."

●●●

Sam was nervous the next morning, but Bobby came through and the CONEX was delivered by 7:45 a.m. Enough ductwork had been neatly stacked and stored by lunchtime that A+ and Five Star were able to begin their work.

By the end of the following week, things looked like they were finally back on track on the second floor, but Sam was as busy as ever. He had guys working everywhere—mechanical equipment was being set on the roof, the glazing contractor and mason were working their way around the east side of the building, and he had plumbers, electricians, fire sprinkler installers, and drywallers working on all three floors. He was hot on the heels of the busiest part of the project, and as he locked up the job on Friday evening, he hoped he'd get in a restful weekend.

Chapter Four

Managing Constraints

Unfortunately, Sam's Monday did not start well.

For starters, he'd promised his wife he'd assemble the baby's crib over the weekend, but he successfully procrastinated long enough that it ended up causing a big argument over dinner on Sunday evening. Then he stayed up way too late to catch the end of the football game, only to watch the Cowboys ultimately lose in overtime—a choice he deeply regretted as soon as he woke up the next morning, when he finally peeled himself out of bed, exhausted, after hitting the snooze button a few too many times. Already running late, when he was halfway to the jobsite he realized he had forgotten his cellphone and had to turn back. He retrieved it and got back on the road, but then his dashboard navigation showed that a huge wreck had unfolded a few miles ahead of him. Sam came to a dead stop and watched the highway turn into a parking lot.

He glanced at the clock on his dash: 6:52 a.m. There was no possible way he was going to make it in time for the huddle. Moving to "plan B," he dialed Gene, but the call went straight to voice-mail. Then it hit him: Gene was stalking that prize buck at his lease this week. He wasn't just off work; he was completely out of range.

Sam felt a surge of panic as he realized no one would be there to open the jobsite. He looked out of his windshield at the sea of cars that hadn't moved, and then called Hank.

"Hey, I'm stuck behind a wreck on 635. I'm hoping I'll be there by 7:30."

"Wow, Sam, *7:30?!* These guys are going to be *mad*. What about the huddle?"

Sam was angry—at Gene's vacation, at whomever caused this traffic, at the stupid Cowboys...but mostly at himself.

"Forget about the huddle today."

"All right," Hank said flatly, unable to hide his disappointment.

Sam finally opened the gate at 7:43 a.m. to a crowd of glowering construction workers. After unlocking the building, giving some orders to the labor foremen, and putting the coffee on, Sam collapsed at his desk. He could not believe the bad luck he was having. He hoped this was just *a bad day* and not the start of *a bad week*. He closed his eyes and pictured himself taking aim at a whitetail in the woods somewhere, but was snapped back to reality when his phone rang.

"Hey, Bobby. What's up?"

"Hey. So, we have a ceiling height issue in the lobby of the main floor. Almost all of Hank's ductwork is wrapped, and my guys are telling me that our ceiling tile won't clear it. Can you come take a look?"

Of course. Another freaking design issue, Sam thought bitterly to himself.

"Sure, be right there."

As Sam went to disconnect the call with Bobby, he received another one, this time from Jim.

"Sam! I guess you're on bankers' hours these days?" Jim joked.

Sam tried to laugh, but he had a hard time disguising his sour mood. "I'm about to suit up and head out to the field," Sam said. "What's going on?"

"It's these restrooms on floors two and three. Something doesn't look right to me. I don't think they'll meet ADA."

"You have to be kidding me!" Sam blurted angrily. "These idiot designers—give me twenty minutes. I need to meet with Bobby in the lobby, then I'm coming."

Sam put on his PPE and was headed to the trailer door when it suddenly swung open, and Roberto almost ran right into him.

"WHOA!" Sam exclaimed.

"Sam! Are you heading out to the site? I have a big problem!" Roberto was breathless.

"Yeah? *Get in line!*" Sam barked.

But Roberto didn't stop. "I was looking at these millwork shops this weekend, and they conflict with half the electrical outlets in the staff lounge on three. They straight cover them up! You know we got them all roughed in, and this is gonna be a lotta re-work if we have to rip them out."

Sam threw his hands up. On a *normal* day he would have gone to his drawings to take a look, but today wasn't a *normal* day— today was *one of those days*. He felt ready to explode. He couldn't remember the last time he'd felt so mad or so frustrated. His head hurt. His stomach hurt. It wasn't even 9:00 a.m. yet and he was already completely out of patience. He was on the verge of taking some of his anger out on Roberto, but he stopped himself.

He had a better idea. He pulled his phone out of his back pocket and scrolled through his contacts. He knew exactly who he was going to call.

● ● ●

Kate Williams was an architect with Cornerstone Partners Design, a full-service architecture studio located on the fifteenth floor of a modern office building in downtown Dallas. She'd been with Cornerstone since graduating near the top of her class from Texas A&M eight years before. Kate had her first internship with Cornerstone her junior year, and she knew early on that she wanted to build a career there. She loved the people, and the culture, and especially that the firm's biggest market was in healthcare. Kate's mom was a Neonatal Intensive Care Unit nurse, and she admired the way her mom fully dedicated herself to helping others. She often worked nights or weekends and wore her concern for her patients home on her face. The medical field had always been meaningful to Kate and she had originally planned on being a doctor, but she couldn't shake the queasiness that always came with anything related to blood.

Her dad, on the other hand, was a master carpenter. He spent weekdays on his business, building elegantly designed and well-appointed custom homes with his small crew of men, and his weekends whistling happily in his workshop as he worked on his dozens of projects. Kate loved to visit with him there, and the smell of the freshly sanded wood. With medicine out of the question, something related to construction also seemed a natural fit. Kate dabbled with architecture in her freshman year and fell in love. She never looked back.

At 8:15 a.m. Kate was sitting at her desk, reviewing some schematic design documents before heading into a meeting, when her phone rang. She looked over and saw that it was Sam Brooks, her superintendent from ProCon Builders at the St. Claire Medical Office Building, which was her first "big" project since her promotion the previous fall, and she smiled. She was enjoying working with him; she was especially glad that he was on this project with her, because she really trusted him.

"Good morning, Sam!" Kate answered brightly. "How are you?"

"Well, thanks for asking Kate!" Sam jeered sarcastically. "I'M REALLY ANGRY!"

Kate was stunned speechless. She'd never heard Sam talk to her, or anyone, like this before. Before she had time to process a response, Sam continued.

"Your drawings are ALL JACKED UP, and now I have MAJOR ISSUES out here onsite!" he ranted. "I need you out here ASAP to help me figure out ALL OF THIS CRAP YOU'VE CREATED!!"

Kate was immediately angered at being spoken to this way, but she didn't understand where this was coming from and so she didn't want to react. She turned to her Outlook and started quickly scanning for an opening in her schedule. Her Monday and Tuesday were nothing but a sea of meetings.

"Sam, I'm in back-to-back design meetings over the next two days. The best I can do is Wednesday morning," Kate replied, wishing she could be out there faster. "Do you mind sending me an email letting me know what's wrong so I can work with you from here?"

"'AN EMAIL'?" Sam yelled. "That is just SO TYPICAL for an architect, Kate! We have REAL ISSUES in the field, and the best YOU can do is 'AN EMAIL'?!"

Sam hung up on her.

"'AN EMAIL'? Can you BELIEVE that?!" He looked out the window at his medical office building, which he now hated and wanted nothing to do with.

Roberto was shocked, and gaped at Sam. He'd never seen Sam behave or talk like this.

Sam turned on his heel, kicked the door open, and stalked towards the field. The rest of the day dragged by miserably. Sam griped and complained and spread his bad mood around to anyone he could attach it to. When the guys started to shut down for the day, he picked up his phone and called Alan.

"I want a beer," Sam said, wasting no time with chit-chat.

"So, it was one of *those* days," Alan stated, knowingly. "Let's meet at the Ice Shack at 5:00."

As far as Sam was concerned, 5:00 p.m. couldn't come sooner.

Alan made his way to the back porch of the Ice Shack and found Sam already waiting for him with a longneck in his hand. The big screen television mounted on the wall near their booth was showing highlights from the Cowboys' miserable loss the night before.

"See the game?" Alan asked.

"Unfortunately."

Sam ranted, starting with the dinnertime spat with his wife and moved on to his lousy commute that morning, after oversleeping and missing the huddle. Alan chuckled sympathetically as Sam wove his tale of woe, and couldn't help but grin as Sam filled him in on all of the jobsite issues he'd experienced that day. Alan had also had plenty of terrible days like that in his long career, and he knew exactly how that felt. However, when Sam got to the part with his phone call to Kate, Alan's smile began to fade.

"...and then I said, 'That's SO TYPICAL of you architects,' and I just hung up on her," Sam finished, feeling pleased with his display of temper.

Alan was disappointed. "Wow, Sam. I can understand your frustration with all the issues that came your way today, but you yelling at the architect like that, and hanging up on her? I mean... well...that's just not the way we do business."

"But, Alan, these architects, *they just don't get it!*" Sam whined. "We're out here in the trenches with these workers and these deadlines, but when there are issues they are *nowhere* to be found!"

"That may be true in some cases, Sam," Alan said sternly, "*but you are the leader on that jobsite.* YOU set the tone. You have to stay *proactive*, not *reactive.*"

Sam grew quiet and thought about what Alan just told him.

"Just follow the golden rule, Sam: '*Treat others as you would want to be treated.*' Did you for a minute try to put yourself in *her* shoes? If you do, you may actually be surprised by what you find out about her—and about yourself." Alan finished his beer and set his empty bottle on the table. There really wasn't much to say after that.

Sam replayed the conversation he had with Kate in his mind. What if *she* hung up on *him*? What if he already had a day planned—could he just drop *everything*?

Sam picked up the tab, sincerely thanked Alan for the "tough love," and then he hit the road. Alan really had him thinking. If he could redo the day, what could he have done to be more *proactive*?

Sam called Jen to let her know that he was going to be late this evening; he was heading back to the job to organize his thoughts. It was 6:45 p.m. when he unlocked the trailer. He grabbed a dry erase marker, went to the whiteboard in the conference room, and started to write. In big black letters at the very top of the whiteboard he wrote the word "*Constraint.*" Underneath that, starting from the left side of the board, he wrote:

Item #1:
What: Ceiling grid clash with ductwork
Where: Main lobby

Item #2

What: Restroom ADA conflict
Where: 2nd/3rd floor

Item #3

What: Electrical outlet/millwork conflict
Where: Staff lounge, 3rd floor

Sam pulled out his notepad and continued down the list, putting every constraint he knew about up on the board. When he'd finished, he checked his watch and it was already 8:00 p.m. He was exhausted, but he realized he felt much better about getting all the issues that had been cataloged in his head and on his notepad condensed to one place: up on the whiteboard in the trailer. It was the first time he had ever done anything like this, and he had to admit he liked seeing all the constraints that were currently impacting work organized in one location. On the way home, he felt determined to be *proactive* on Tuesday, and find solutions to these issues.

●●●

Sam did not oversleep Tuesday morning; in fact, he was up and out the door with his Thermos of coffee forty-five minutes earlier than usual. He picked up a couple dozen sausage kolaches for the guys, and then got settled in with his laptop and his breakfast to check his email.

He had a message from Kate Williams with Cornerstone Partners Design:

Sam,

I think we got disconnected yesterday, but I wanted to follow up and let you know that I rearranged my schedule for today. I can be onsite at 1:00 this afternoon to help find solutions to whatever problems you're experiencing and support you in the field. Let me know if that time doesn't work.

Kate

Sam was relieved that Kate was coming out to help fix the issues on the job, but he also felt guilty for the way he'd treated her the day before. He knew he needed to apologize.

At 7:00 a.m., Sam started the huddle by telling everyone that he wanted to use the time to focus on the constraints that he'd listed on the wall. Bobby was the first to go, and Sam pointed to "Item #1" on the board which read:

Item #1:
What: Ceiling grid clash with ductwork
Where: Main lobby

"Oh, yeah..." Bobby started slowly. "About that. Uh, sorry, Hank, that one is on me. My acoustical foreman somehow got ahold of the original bid set's reflected ceiling plan and did not have the updated ASI number one, which added the furr-down and lowered the soft ceiling by three inches, in turn giving us *plenty* of room to clear the bottom of the duct."

"So, you're saying we have no issue with ceiling height in the lobby? Is that right?" Sam asked, and Bobby confirmed that was the case.

"All right!" Hank cheered. "Scratch it off the list!"

Sam was happy to see the first issue resolved so quickly, but he was also a bit frustrated that Bobby did not do his homework before immediately calling him yesterday with his "the sky is falling" issue.

"Hey, Bobby, can you make sure you run these kinds of things to the ground before bringing it forward to me or the team? It would help my blood pressure!" he teased, though still a bit annoyed.

Bobby was a little embarrassed. "Fair enough."

Jim was up next, and Sam pointed to "Item #2" on the constraint board which read:

Item #2
What: Restroom ADA conflict
Where: 2nd/3rd floor

"Yeah Sam, about that..." Jim began sheepishly. "When I called you, I thought the restrooms off the west side of the atrium on the second and third floors were public restrooms, with the sinks in casework. If that was the case, they would not meet ADA. But after we talked, I double-checked the architectural blow-ups of the restrooms and our submittals, and realized they are staff restroom, not public. The staff restrooms have wall-hung sinks, which clear ADA. Sorry about that. Honest mistake," he finished.

Sam took a deep breath. He was trying not to appear as irritated as he felt. He looked at the group and said, "Guys, again, as a rule of thumb, please bird-dog these issues and make sure you actually have one before getting me involved."

As he turned and looked at Roberto to indicate that it was his turn, it hit him: the last time he saw Roberto was in the trailer, right after he blew up and hung up on Kate.

Oh no, he thought, with a sinking feeling. *I didn't chase any of these things down before calling and yelling at Kate. I'm guilty of doing this myself.*

Then Alan's voice played in his head: *Be proactive, Sam, not reactive!*

Roberto began to discuss "Item #3" on the board:

Item #3
What: Electrical outlet/millwork conflict
Where: Staff lounge, 3rd floor

"This constraint is still open, Sam," Roberto began. "I think I understand the issue better now, though," he added, wanting to make sure Sam knew he did some due diligence. "The electrical drawings and the architectural drawings don't match. There is no millwork shown on our drawings, so we have outlets at sixteen inches off the floor," he explained. "On the architectural drawings they show casework, so it looks like the outlets should have been measured from the countertops. I hate that we didn't catch this before we installed!" he concluded, shaking his head. "It's just that my guys tend to only look at the electrical prints and forget to review the architecturals."

"I see," Sam replied. "I do have some good news to share, Roberto, and that is that the architect will be out here today at 1:00 p.m., and I'll be sure to have her look into it."

Roberto looked at Sam and then at the constraint board. "I like this board, Sam, but it's missing who's responsible for resolving the constraints."

Roberto went to the board, added a row for "*Who*" with his dry erase marker, and then added Kate's name:

Item #3
What: Electrical outlet/millwork conflict
Where: Staff lounge, 3rd floor
Who: Kate Williams (Cornerstone)

As the team went over the remaining constraints before their fifteen minutes were up, they populated the "*Who*" area for all outstanding items. Some constraints were due to ProCon Builders, some were waiting on a decision by the owner, and some constraints, such as procurement issues affecting work, were caused by the trades themselves.

As the huddle ended and the guys made their way back to their crews, Sam felt really energized by the progress they made in the meeting. The whiteboard detailing the constraints had an impact on the entire team that he didn't expect, and he agreed with Roberto that it did make sense to list who was responsible for getting an issue resolved. It added the weight of accountability directly onto the person whose name was listed next to a constraint. He finished the morning by making his rounds, completing his safety checklist, and making sure the composite clean-up crews had the building looking neat and orderly.

●●●

Sam had just finished the burrito that he'd ordered off the lunch truck when Kate Williams came through the door of his trailer at 1:00 p.m., on the dot, as promised. She was dressed in her blue jeans, safety vest, Cornerstone Partners Design logo hard hat, and safety glasses.

Arm outstretched, she shook Sam's hand firmly. "Hey, Sam," she said with a smile, but she sounded a little more serious than usual. "Looks like you guys have been busy!"

"We sure have!" Sam said, trying to sound relaxed. He felt uncomfortable about the conversation he knew he needed to have next.

"Listen, Kate, before we get started, I need to apologize to you for my call yesterday."

Kate said nothing and listened.

"I was *way* out of line. I was having a really bad day, and I was a complete jerk to you when I called. That's NOT our culture at ProCon Builders, and definitely not the way I usually communicate."

Kate looked relieved. Sam continued, "If I could do it again, the call I would have made would be to ask if you would be willing to do a weekly walk with me to review some field issues."

"Apology accepted!" Kate answered quickly. "Sam, I hope you know that I want this project to be a success as badly as you do. I know that contractors can't stand it when the drawings are incorrect—and architects can't stand it when a contractor builds something that's not per the plans, or isn't with the specified materials. But if we communicate regularly, and can have trust that we both have the project's best interests in mind, I believe we can be a strong team and turn over a building that both of us will be proud of."

Sam liked the sound of that. "Deal!" he said with a smile, and they shook hands again. He paused a moment and then spontaneously added, "I want you to come take a look at something." Sam gestured for her to follow him into the trailer's conference room.

Sam knew that he would usually be more reserved with the information he would share with an architect, but he was thinking about what Kate just said. If they were really going to be a team, he might as well pull back the curtain and be as transparent as he could.

Sam spread his hands before the whiteboard and said, "Kate, this details every constraint we are currently tracking on this project. Now, some of these are issues we see with the prints, some of these are items we are waiting for direction on, and some of these are our own mistakes or problems we are facing with getting materials onsite. In the spirit of being a team, I'm sharing with you the list that keeps me up at night."

Kate started reading over the list and, for the first time, really understood the stress that Sam was under. She turned to him and said, "Let's try to knock some of this stuff out!"

●●●

Kate and Sam spent two hours together, walking every square inch of the project. They reviewed conflicts in the field, discussed quality control issues, and even got to know each other a bit better. It turned out that Kate was a huge Cowboys fan, just like Sam, and that they both liked to fly fish.

When their walk was finished, they went back to revisit the constraint board. Sam handed Kate a water bottle, and they took a couple of minutes to review everything that was written there.

"There's just one thing missing from your board, Sam," Kate said, uncapping a dry erase maker.

She wrote the word "*When*." Then she went to the items that had her name beside them, and wrote a date to make it an official commitment.

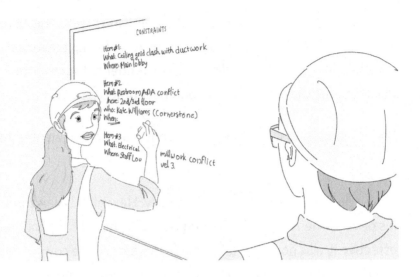

Sam loved this idea. "This is terrific, Kate. I can't tell you how much I really appreciate your time today." Kate shared that she was surprised by how much she'd learned and how impressed she was by the progress in the field. They agreed to meet again the following week.

Over the next few days, Sam incorporated the constraint board as part of the daily huddle meeting, and he marveled at how effective it was. He remembered that, before he started using it, the trades used to find him or call him throughout the day with their problems, and he would have to go from issue to issue, trade foreman to trade foreman, to help get them resolved. But now, with the constraint board, the trades would populate the issues themselves and then begin to work on their problems with each other, face-to-face after the meeting. This was such an improvement.

Late Friday morning, Alan called Sam to let him know he was putting together an agenda for the monthly superintendent huddle, which was scheduled for the following week. This huddle was something Alan had created a few years back; it involved bringing all of ProCon Builders' superintendents together to discuss safety, lessons learned, and best practices.

"I was wondering if you had any lessons learned you wanted to share?"

"I sure do!" Sam replied enthusiastically. He walked Alan through his development of the constraint board on his jobsite, and how effective it was now that all of the constraints were completely visible to the entire team. He explained how the entire team—including the project architect—helped flesh out the board by adding who was responsible and when the constraint was going to be resolved.

Alan was extremely impressed. "Wow! And it's working well? The guys are bought in?"

"You wouldn't believe it!" Sam replied. "The impact is huge. It has really taken the huddle to another level."

"Sam, it's amazing how far you have come in such a short amount of time! Next time you're in my area I want you to stop by my site. There's something I want to show you."

They ended the call, and Sam walked over to his trailer window to look out at his project. He watched as dozens of different subcontractors moved through their work and he smiled, feeling gratified. Even though he still had lost time to make up and it was going to be a tough push through finishes, Sam loved the direction his project was moving in, and he was very optimistic.

Chapter Five

Pull Planning

"...and while you might need a jacket this morning, you can expect our lunchtime temps to be in the lower-to-mid-sixties, with sun and clear skies. No rain today, but that will change as we approach the weekend with a seventy percent chance of precipitation starting early on Saturday. Evening drive time should be..."

Sam killed his truck's engine and clicked on his phone. Photos of the crib, assembled and carefully painted that weekend, were accumulating "likes" by the dozens from friends and family on his wife's social media. The baby was due in about fifteen weeks, and Sam and Jen alternated between feelings of terror and joy. He pictured his tiny baby sleeping in that crib, and he smiled. It was 6:02 a.m.—he was an hour early, and he felt grateful for the good weather and his peaceful weekend, because he had a very big day ahead of him.

A few weeks earlier, Bobby had pulled Sam aside and suggested holding a safety appreciation lunch for the guys in the field; he thought it would help boost morale and show appreciation for their successful dedication to zero lost-time incidents onsite. Sam thought this was a great idea, and he got together with Gene to discuss dates and a budget.

That's when the snowball began to roll.

Not really expecting him to come, Gene politely invited his boss, who didn't just *accept*—he turned around and invited the entire leadership team at ProCon Builders, who then invited the entire Planning, Design, and Construction team at St. Claire Health System's North Texas Division, plus all of the senior principals at Cornerstone Design Partners. Before Gene and Sam knew it, what started off as a simple safety appreciation lunch for the tradesmen had turned into a massive, project-wide celebration with wall-to-wall executives. There was even going to be a keynote speaker—the CEO of the entire St. Claire Health System, Dr. Chelsea Harrison.

When Gene told Sam the news, Sam felt butterflies in his stomach. On one hand, this was the kind of project he always dreamed of building: one that was important to a lot of people, and one that he could be proud to show to his kids someday. But, on the other hand, this was now going to be a much bigger event than he'd anticipated, and he was worried about all of the attention (and eyes) that would be on him and on his project.

And today was the day. He knew he had to make it a success.

Sam started the coffee and then met with his labor foremen to make sure they would have the building neat as a pin and ready for their dozens of important visitors. He then caught up on his daily reports in case any higher-ups asked to see them, gathered up the door prizes he'd bought the night before to raffle off to the subcontractors, and neatly laid out rows of new hard hats and a stack of vests.

At the huddle that morning, he prepped the foremen for the day and made sure they were ready to work with the event company, which was scheduled to arrive at 9:00 a.m. to put up tents and set up tables and chairs. He double-checked with Roberto to make sure he had temporary power ready to go for the microphones and speakers, and then called the caterer to verify that they were good to go.

Gene arrived at 10:30 a.m., and they walked the site together to confirm that everything was perfect. By 11:30, everyone had made it through the buffet line, which was loaded with fajitas and all of the fixings, plus rice, beans, and chips with salsa. Sam waited until noon before he asked for everyone's attention, and he began the festivities by thanking everyone for coming out to celebrate their 50,000 man-hours to-date with zero lost-time injuries. Roberto stood next to him, translating what he was saying for the Spanish-speaking craftsmen. After the applause died down, Gene said a few words and then introduced one of the directors from St. Claire's PDC group, who pulled a folded sheet of paper from his pocket and began his introduction of Dr. Chelsea Harrison, St. Claire Health System's CEO.

"Established in Dallas–Fort Worth forty-five years ago, St. Claire provides a full range of family care as well as fifteen specialty and sub-specialty healthcare services from nine campuses throughout the southern United States. Dr. Harrison came to St. Claire six years ago, bringing with her more than twenty years of healthcare administration experience where she has led institutions across the country in the application of performance management, process improvement, healthcare operations, and strategy. Under her incredible leadership, St. Claire has acquired or opened four new hospitals and increased revenue from 850 million dollars to more than two billion dollars. The facility we are all visiting today will spearhead another exciting era of growth for St. Claire here on our original campus in North Texas. Dr. Harrison's guidance has facilitated the expansion of our services, our geographic reach, and St. Claire's mission to provide quality healthcare to all members of the communities that we serve," he said. "At this time, Dr. Harrison would like to say a few words."

While the crowd applauded, she approached the podium and shook his hand, put on her glasses, and cleared her throat.

"Thank you," she began. "Ladies and gentlemen, it's a great honor for me, and all of us at St. Claire Health System, to be here with you today to celebrate the health and well-being of the men and women who are working so hard each day to create the facilities that will provide essential health care services for so many of our loved ones in this wonderful community. Thank you for the diligence and attention to detail that has contributed to your accomplishments towards safety on this important jobsite."

Everyone clapped again, including some loud whistles from the drywallers in the back.

"The medical office building currently under construction..." she continued, gesturing to the construction site visible in the distance over her left shoulder, "...will allow all of the administrative functions in the main hospital to relocate, subsequently freeing up much-needed space to open more beds and increase patient loads, allowing us to better serve our neighbors in need."

Dr. Harrison went on for a couple of minutes to speak in more detail about the other areas of work, the eventual campus expansion, and its impact on the St. Claire system and the North Texas community, and concluded her remarks by saying, "Thank you again for allowing us to be part of your celebration today, and I look forward to rejoining you here for the ribbon-cutting in June."

As Roberto finished translating, he turned around and shot Sam a puzzled look. As people were leaving, Bobby came up to Sam and said, "Ribbon-cutting in *June*, huh? Interesting that your schedule shows it in *May*. Suddenly we have *an extra month*?" he asked sarcastically. "I've been telling you *for weeks* that I'm worried we are behind schedule. I've put pressure on my crews and lost sleep, and you've known all along we've had this extra time?! Unbelievable!"

Sam felt his face grow hot with a mixture of embarrassment and anger. "Your schedule is whatever I tell you it is!" he snapped. The words shot out of his mouth before he was able to think, and more aggressively then he'd intended.

Bobby shook his head and walked away. As Sam watched him leave, he thought back to his first project as a superintendent; he'd turned it over a week late, and he was chewed out pretty badly for it. It was a painful lesson, and from that Sam learned that the super had to make, maintain, and own the schedule—no matter what. Even if the end product was great quality, a missed schedule was something that an owner would not forgive or forget, and it could cost you your job.

The problem with construction is that so many things were completely outside of your control—anything from local weather to political crap in Washington could impact your material deliveries, or labor onsite, and beyond. So, about five years ago, Sam started running two schedules: one for the field, and one for the project managers to share with the clients. On this project, the schedule he was pushing on the field showed them completing a month earlier than what was actually scheduled, and Sam liked it just fine that way. This way, if something went wrong, he had some buffer.

This was the first time he had been "caught" in the white lie of dual schedules.

Oh well, he thought. *That's just the way our business is.*

At the huddle the next morning, Sam could feel an icy chill in the room.

"What a great safety celebration!" Sam tried, with exaggerated enthusiasm. "The feedback I got from our C-suite at ProCon Builders was great!"

The room was stone quiet. None of the foremen said anything. When the egg timer was set, Bobby went to the board and immediately started complaining.

"We were supposed to have all of these walls drywalled by next Friday and it's not going to happen. We've had to wait too much on plumbing and electrical in-wall partials, and I don't have the manpower to accelerate." Bobby capped his marker and rejoined the group, signaling that he was done discussing the matter.

Roberto laughed and tried to provoke Bobby, saying, "If your guys weren't so slow, you'd be able to make it—but you drywallers spend all your time complaining!"

"Whoa, whoa, whoa," Sam butted in, holding his hands up. "Guys, what is going on this morning? We're a team, remember?"

"'A team'?" Bobby asked incredulously, fixing his eyes on Sam. "You've been cracking the whip on us for the last three months— and *for what?*"

"So he can FINISH a month EARLY!" Roberto accused, loudly.

"Well, in the spirit of being 'a team,' we have some news for you, too, Sam," Jim spat. "None of us ever believed we could hit May in the first place! And by the looks of it, June may be a stretch!"

"This isn't 'a team,' Sam," Bobby said, angrily. "You're just like every other general contractor out there."

"He's right," Tom agreed, frowning at Sam. "You think you have all the answers, and you don't have a clue."

"You're lying to yourself, Sam. This project has been easily five to six weeks behind schedule, and even with us getting these four weeks back, we're still behind the eight ball by a couple of weeks," Bobby announced. "You *lied* to us about our completion date, you *pushed* these fake milestones on us—and we're supposed to just sit back and tell you whatever you want to hear? Yeah, I'm not going to do that."

"I'm not working this way, and I'm done with these daily huddles," Hank declared, tossing his dry erase marker on the table. He put on his hard hat and stormed out of the trailer. Roberto followed him, and so did Tom and Bobby, and all of the other foremen.

Sam found himself standing alone. Strong emotions were racing through him—anger, confusion, humiliation. He couldn't believe their nerve, walking out of his meeting that way! He wanted to tell the guys off. But on the other hand, he couldn't help but wonder if they were right. Should he have lied about the completion date? Was he lying to himself? Didn't he keep saying that they were a team—and was he treating them like part of a team if he wasn't being honest?

Sam picked up the phone and called Alan.

"Hey, Sam! How are you?" Alan answered cheerfully, but before Sam could respond he continued, "Sounds like you had a great showing yesterday on your project. I heard the higher-ups were impressed!"

Sam thanked him half-heartedly. His mind was on the failed huddle.

"Uh-oh, everything all right?" Alan asked.

"I need to get your thoughts on something," Sam began. "At the event yesterday, it came out that the ribbon-cutting ceremony is going to happen in June. The problem is the schedule I've got the field pushing towards shows us being done in *May*. The guys heard this yesterday, and now they're mad. This morning, they told me that, even after learning about the extra month, we're still further behind than maybe I allowed myself to realize. And then they all walked out on the huddle! I still can't believe it."

"I see," acknowledged Alan, who was waiting to hear what Sam would say next.

"So, I was calling to ask you—has this happened to you before? I'm thinking about asking Gene to set up meetings with each trade's office to tell them that if they don't hit our May schedule then they might not get work on future phases. What're your thoughts? Too harsh?"

Silence.

Sam thought maybe they'd been disconnected. "Alan?"

"Listen, Sam, you've been making great progress out there, but I have to tell you I'm surprised that you think this is the right approach. Remember, without team alignment none of the tools you're using to help your project will get you as far as you'd like. You made big strides with your architect, but you need to realize the subcontractors are a huge part of the team. You need their buy-in and expertise; otherwise, you could be heading up that famous creek without a paddle."

Sam was embarrassed, and felt a bit unfairly judged. "You've never been caught between two schedules?"

"Sam, I don't have two schedules. On my projects, the trades and the client have the exact same schedule. There are no secrets between us. In fact, we make the schedule together."

Now it was Sam's turn to be silent. He'd never heard of this kind of thing before.

"Hey, have you heard of pull planning before?" Alan asked. Sam admitted he hadn't, and Alan smiled to himself. He thought this was one of the most powerful tools he used in the field, and he was excited to share it.

"Tell you what, why don't you and Gene take a trip out here Friday morning? We're having a small milestone pull plan session with some trades at 9:00 a.m., and I'd like to go over some things with you boys before then. Bring your notepad and an open mind, and I'll see you in Fort Worth at 7:00 a.m. sharp."

●●●

Sam arranged for another superintendent to watch his site Friday, and he and Gene rode together to Fort Worth. His week had not improved; most of the foremen had completely stopped coming to the huddle, and Sam now felt isolated and disliked most of the time. He missed the easy banter, and especially the collaboration he once took for granted with his trades. But he was relieved to have a break from his stressful jobsite.

As he walked into the conference room at ProCon Builders' triple-wide trailer for the Trinity Grove Specialty Hospital project, he was amazed by what he saw on the walls. There were the now-familiar floor plans under laminate, but there was MUCH more that he didn't recognize. A huge, detailed schedule showing the upcoming six weeks, a "material delivery" board, an "inspection" board, a board that had two kinds of charts—a pie chart and one with a jagged line, and a huge calendar board with empty boxes and lines between them. Sam and Gene spent a few minutes studying all of these items while they waited for Alan, who was taking a call in his office.

"Good morning, fellas!" Alan said, greeting them warmly, and putting one hand each on Sam's and Gene's shoulders. "Glad you could make it."

"Thanks for letting us join you today," Gene said.

"What is all of this?" Sam asked, wide-eyed.

"This is our Big Room," Alan said proudly. "There's a lot here to talk about, and we'll get to all of it in time, but today we're just going to focus on pull planning."

Alan approached the whiteboard and wrote the words *Push* and *Pull*. Gene and Sam started taking notes as he talked. "Now, Gene, I know you like fancy coffee, so I'll use you in my example for *push*."

Sam pointed at Gene's ubiquitous Mojo Java cup and laughed.

"In a *push* environment, a firm produces goods without a real regard for actual customer demand. So, for our example, let's imagine you walked into a Mojo Java store and learned that they'd decided to brew the entire day's coffee based off a forecast of how many people they thought would come that day. That would be considered *push*, and the problem with *push* is that forecasts can be inaccurate. Maybe they made too much, and they won't sell all of that coffee—or, on the other hand, maybe they didn't make enough, and now some people won't get any."

"And poor Gene would have to go a day without his gingerbread-house macchio-whatever!" Sam joked. Gene, having not anticipated being the butt of jokes so early in the morning, frowned.

"Exactly!" said Alan, who was pretending not to notice Gene's displeasure. "There could be wasted inventory or shortages. But in *pull* production, no work is done until a customer's order is placed. So, when Gene orders his gran-dee cotton candy latte, that triggers the Mojo Java employee…"

"The *barista*," Gene corrected, and then turned red.

"Oh, sorry, the *barista*…" Alan corrected with a grin, "…to begin the process of making and pouring the coffee. The advantage is that you don't have to worry about coffee being wasted or storing an inventory of brewed coffee—if that were a thing. Does any of this make sense?"

Gene and Sam sat quietly, still a bit confused.

"OK," Alan said, "let's try this. Sam, do you fill up your truck with gas every morning and every evening?"

"No, I get gas when my empty light turns on," Sam replied.

Alan nodded. "That is *pull*. You're filling up only when there is a demand."

"All right," said Sam, "I think I understand the difference, but what does this have to do with scheduling?"

"I'm glad you asked! Gene, when was the last time you flew somewhere for vacation?"

Gene thought. "Last winter. My family and I flew to Wyoming to ski in Jackson Hole."

"That sounds fun!" said Sam, who'd never been skiing.

"It was fun, but it was hectic, too. It was the first time we'd flown with our toddler. We ran so late that we almost missed our flight leaving town."

Alan laughed. "I bet that's something most people can relate to, and I'm happy that you mentioned it because it'll help with this exercise."

Alan walked to the end of the table where he had several neat stacks of differently colored sticky notepads and a pile of markers. He took one pad of sticky notes and two markers and gave them to Gene and Sam.

"Now, I want you guys to think about every activity involved in the process of going to the airport to board a flight, but I want you to start with the *last step* in the process—boarding the plane—and work your way backwards to the part where you're getting your things together to leave your house. Write each one of them down on a sticky note for me."

Gene and Sam glanced at each other, not quite sure where this was going.

"Come on, this isn't hard!" coaxed Alan.

Sam and Gene uncapped their pens and started collaborating. As they talked, they completed six separate sticky notes and Alan placed them on the whiteboard as they worked:

- Walk to the gate
- Get through security
- Get boarding pass & check bag
- Park and get shuttle
- Drive to the airport
- Pack suitcase

Gene had started filling out another card with *get suitcase out of the attic*, but Alan stopped him and told him that what they'd already done was plenty.

"OK, this is great. Next step, I need you to write down a time frame for how long you expect each one of these activities to take."

Gene and Sam went to the whiteboard and they wrote a duration on each sticky:

- Walk to the gate = 5 minutes
- Get through security = 20 minutes
- Get boarding pass & check bag = 15 minutes
- Park and get shuttle = 15 minutes
- Drive to the airport = 20 minutes
- Pack suitcase = 15 minutes

"Perfect," Alan said. "Now, if you'll notice, almost every activity has a hand-off, or predecessor, meaning *the thing that comes before it*. In other words, it's what has to happen before the next thing can be done. For example, in order to walk to the gate, you have to get through security. Before you can go through security, you need to have a boarding pass and check your bag. Are you following me?"

"Yeah, it makes sense," Sam replied. Gene nodded in agreement.

"It's the same way in our construction schedules. In order for you to two-side walls, you need to have your electrical and plumbing rough-in inspection. To get those inspections, the rough-in has to be complete. In order for rough-in to be complete, the stud walls have to be in place. Understanding the hand-offs between activities is important.

"Now, back to our airport story. Let me ask you this, Sam: if you need to be on your plane this morning at 8:30 a.m., what time should you be packing your suitcase?"

Sam quickly added up the minutes on the sticky notes and said, "The whole process takes an hour and a half, so 7:00 a.m."

"Sorry, Sam, but *it's 7:30*," Alan said, pointing at his watch. "Now what?"

"You'd better haul ass, Sam!" Gene joked. Sam and Alan laughed.

"Seriously, though, what's your plan?" Alan coaxed. "How are you going to make the flight?"

Sam thought for a moment, and then grabbed the sticky pad. He wrote down *Taxi = 20 minutes* on one card, and then *Electronic boarding pass & carry-on bag = 2 minutes* on another.

Then he walked to the whiteboard and took down the cards that read:

- Get boarding pass & check bag = 15 minutes
- Park and get shuttle = 15 minutes
- Drive to the airport = 20 minutes

and replaced them with the two new ones he'd made. He studied the new list for a moment, and then Gene walked over to join him. Gene peeled off the note reading *Walk to the gate = 5 minutes* and replaced it with *Run to the gate = 3 minutes*.

Now the sticky notes looked like this:

- Run to the gate = 3 minutes
- Get through security = 20 minutes

- Electronic boarding pass & carry-on bag = 2 minutes
- Taxi = 20 minutes
- Pack suitcase = 15 minutes

"Well done!" said Alan. "You realized you weren't going to make schedule, so you looked at each hand-off and found a different way to 'skin the cat'. What would be so hard about doing this on your project?"

"What do you mean?" asked Sam.

"Well, you're here because your trades have told you they can't make your schedule, right? So, make it *their schedule*. You know your Certificate of Occupancy date, don't you? Bring those guys in a room, have them identify all the activities with durations—from the end of the job until now—and how each one of those activities hands off to the next. Just like when you found out you should have started packing thirty minutes sooner, you need to find out how long ago you should have started two-siding walls. Then have the team look at each hand-off and see if there is a better way to cut time. Maybe the phasing is off, or maybe there are constraints you can remove. How will you know if you don't ask them for input?"

Sam sat down. It was finally becoming crystal clear to him. Up until this point, all he had ever done was *push* a schedule— without any input from anyone else—based on a forecast of what he thought could be done. How could he have not seen it earlier?

"Are you OK?" asked Gene, who was watching Sam.

Sam looked at Alan. "This has been eye-opening for me." He shook his head. "It seems so simple...yet hard."

Alan laughed. "It's both."

"Well, how do we start?" Gene asked, taking a seat of his own.

"Guys, the way you start is by first understanding that your subcontractors are your partners. Believe me, I spent the first twenty-five years of my career believing that, as project superintendent for ProCon Builders, I was the *leader* on my job and the subcontractors were *followers*. It used to be 'my way or the highway,' as they say. That was the way I came up in the business. When I was starting out, only the general contractor superintendents were fully engaged—thinking, observing, analyzing, and problem-solving. The rest of us kept our heads down and our mouths shut and just did what we were told." Alan chuckled and shook his head.

"But what I have learned is that we are so much better with *everyone* participating—everyone in the field having a voice, empowered to make decisions, and being accountable. I think that once you realize that, you won't believe how well your projects will run, the relationships you'll make, and the improvement of morale on your site."

As Alan talked, he poured cups of fresh coffee and handed them to Gene and Sam.

"I don't even refer to the trades as *subcontractors* anymore. It just doesn't sit right with me; the word 'sub' sounds...I don't know.

Belittling. Most of the work put in place on our jobs is done by our trades, and to me 'sub' doesn't represent that. These are smart, talented people who know their craft better than I ever could. I call them *trade partners*, and I think partnership means shared leadership. Leaders are respected individuals who are empowered to build consensus and resolve conflict."

What on Earth could Sam say to that? He took a sip of his coffee and stared at all of the strange charts and lists on display in Alan's Big Room. He felt disoriented, like his perspective on his job had been turned completely upside-down. Sam could see that Alan was right, on so many levels. The fact that Alan was taking him to school right now made him feel like such a dumb rookie, but also just really lucky to be mentored by someone with such a unique approach to building. Sam hadn't ever heard anyone in construction talk this way before.

Gene smiled. "Alan, you make me feel proud to work for ProCon Builders."

Sam was invigorated and sprung to his feet. "I'm sold—on the whole freaking thing!" Sam said, spreading his arms wide. "All of this stuff. I want to know *everything*."

Alan smiled broadly. "Well, you're in luck!" he laughed. "In about ten minutes, we're having a pull plan meeting in this room. We're adding a 15,000 square foot administration building on this campus as part of our next phase, and this morning we're pulling to the milestone of having the foundation poured. Can you guys stay for a couple of hours?" Sam and Gene nodded.

"Great! OK, before the others get here, let me tell you a few ground rules to make these pull plan sessions effective. You might want to take some notes so it's easier to remember," Alan prompted. Sam and Gene reached for their notepads.

"The first thing is to make sure everyone understands the purpose of the pull plan meeting. Our goal for today's meeting is two-fold. We want the trade partners to—number one—*plan collaboratively*, and we want them to—number two—*commit to the tasks, durations, and hand-offs between them*. A week ago, we notified the trades that we were going to run a pull session today, moving back from the milestone of foundation complete. So they could come ready, we asked that they prepare ahead of time, giving some good thought into what activities they'll have, how long it'll take to complete those activities, and what constraints may be in their way."

The men proceeded to discuss the logistics of an effective pull planning meeting. Sam asked who needed to attend, and Alan described how important it is that the foremen who oversee the execution of the work with their craftsmen be in attendance. He explained that a trade partner's office staff could attend if they had knowledge of material procurement and fabrication, but to make sure that the only people in the meeting were the ones who brought value and had the authority to make a commitment to the team.

Gene asked what supplies were needed, and Alan gestured to the room. "First, you need an adequate space. We call this our Big Room, and the Big Room's purpose is to support cross-functional team collaboration. The culture in the Big Room is that there are no badges. Everyone has an equal voice and we are focused on collaborative planning, problem-solving, and team-building."

Besides adequate space, Alan explained that the other required items were:

- Several different colors of sticky notepads (a different color for each trade) and enough markers for the trades to write down their activities, durations, and hand-offs;

- Somewhere to place the sticky notes, like a whiteboard;

- A big sheet of paper, or some separate whiteboard space, to capture *constraints* (issues that need to be resolved to release work) and a *parking lot* (the items that need to be discussed, but do not directly impact the schedule or need everyone's involvement in the room);

- Documents like drawings and specs, site plans, floor plans, and other visual communication documents for the trades to refer to when planning; and

- A printed copy of the project's master schedule for transparency and to reference.

After Sam and Gene finished jotting down this information, Sam asked how much time ideally needed to be set aside for a pull planning meeting. Alan advised allowing two-to-three hours, saying that this time spent collaborating was time well spent, and stressed that it was important not to rush and risk leaving out critical items that could affect the schedule. However, on the other hand, taking too much time could make it difficult to maintain full engagement from the team. A key to success is to make sure the time commitment and the expectations for all of the participants are made very clear in advance.

They were wrapping up their logistics discussion as the first trade partners began to enter the room.

"All right!" Alan said, taking a deep breath and rubbing his hands together with excitement. "Are you ready to watch your first pull plan?"

● ● ●

The trades seemed to know the drill well as they began to help themselves to sticky pads and markers before getting coffee and finding a seat. Alan welcomed everyone and asked them to introduce themselves by name and company. He then reminded the team of the intent of the meeting, clearly communicating the pull plan process and his expectations for the team around communication and commitments.

Over the next hour, trades began to fill out their cards. Sam and Gene observed the trades asking each other questions, going to the visual communication tools to discuss logistics, and writing down their constraints on the pull plan's constraint board. Alan worked his way around the room, answering questions and making sure the team added enough detail on each card. He explained that, if someone who did not attend the session read the card, they should be able to easily understand the activity.

Alan also made sure no durations took longer than ten days. He told the trades that if a duration is longer than ten days, he wanted them to break it into multiple cards to allow succeeding activities to begin sooner, which would optimize the schedule. He also made sure to tell the trades that he did not want them to add any buffer or float to their durations; sandbagging could have major impacts to the schedule, and he challenged a few of the trades when he saw durations that seemed longer then they should be. Sometimes they agreed, and sometimes they were able to make their case, but in both situations, they came to resolution.

At around 10:00 a.m., Alan told the team it was time to start putting the sticky notes up on the board and reminded them that each card signified *the completion of the activity*, not *the start*. The trades' cards were in "swim lanes," one for each trade: earthwork, concrete, plumbing, and electrical. Sam and Gene watched as Alan helped the trades through the first few hand-offs until it seemed as if everyone was comfortable with the flow, and then the participants started placing the stickies themselves while having conversations regarding their needs and commitments.

At one point, the concrete foreman stubbornly told the electrical and plumbing foremen that he did not want them in his way while he was installing piers or grade beams. He turned to Alan and said, "If I don't have any plumbers and electricians doing underground in my way, I could have all the piers and grade beams done on this building in twenty days—but with them in my way, it will take me thirty days."

Alan studied the electrical and plumbing stickies, which added up to fifteen days of underground.

"OK...so, if they wait until you are completely done, the total duration is your twenty days *plus* fifteen days...which is thirty-five days," Alan began. "But, if their hand-off is when you finish *piers*, not *grade beams*, it may take you thirty days, but *their* fifteen days starts on *your* day fifteen, which *pulls the total duration to thirty days*. Which means we accelerate by a week."

"Huh, that may actually help us with manpower, since we're tight," the concrete foreman mused. "I commit to having two more weeks," he added quickly, worried that Alan may change his mind.

"And I like having five days less on the overall schedule," Alan reassured.

At the end of the session, everyone verbally committed to the durations on the board. Alan took photos of the pull boards, constraints, and parking lot items, and promised the team that he would issue a six-week look-ahead schedule capturing the commitments and send it out at the beginning of the following week. As the trades left the Big Room to head to lunch, Alan turned to Gene and Sam and asked what they thought.

"Impressive," said Gene.

Sam nodded. "Unreal. Everyone was engaged and looked confident that they had a schedule they could achieve. I do have a question, though: what was the part at the end, about the 'six-week look-ahead'?"

Alan grinned. "Sam, what you just witnessed, pull planning, is just one component of something called the Last Planner System."

"Oh, Last Planner System? What's that?" Sam asked, pulling out his notepad.

Alan, laughed. "There will be plenty of time for that some other day. Right now, you guys look hungry—and I'm pretty sure I look hungry, too. There's an awesome burger place down the street we can walk to. Sound good?"

•••

Sam and Gene toured Alan's project after lunch, and then Sam climbed in his truck to head to his jobsite. On the way there he called Bobby, who was polite but not exactly friendly on the call. Things still hadn't gone back to normal since the safety celebration kerfuffle.

"Hey, Bobby, I was wondering if you and the other foremen had time for a cold drink at the Ice Shack after work. How's 4:00 p.m.?"

"Ice Shack? So, that's where you've been all day," Bobby snarked. "I don't know, Sam, it's been a long week..."

"Please, Bobby," Sam interrupted. "I've got something on my mind. It would really mean a lot to me. I'll buy."

Bobby reluctantly agreed to try and rally the group for happy hour and a conversation. When he arrived at the Ice Shack, he had Hank, Roberto, Jim, and Tom with him. Sam waved them over to the large table he'd secured.

"Hey, I really appreciate you guys coming," said Sam, smiling.

"Bobby said you were buying, so I wasn't going to miss an opportunity to run up your tab!" Roberto joked.

Sam laughed. "Fair enough!"

After ordering pitchers and appetizers, the guys talked about their plans for the weekend to break the ice. Before long, Bobby turned to Sam and said, "All right, I feel like you're buttering us up for something, and I'm betting it's not good. So, let's go ahead and get on with it."

Sam pulled a folded piece of paper out of his front pocket and spread it out on the table before them. It was his project schedule.

"Oh boy," Tom groaned, rolling his eyes. "Here we go."

But before anyone else could talk, Sam spoke. "Fellas, I owe you an apology."

The men shot quick glances at each other.

"As you know, I haven't been honest with you about our completion date. Today, that changes. I want you guys to know that I respect all of you and value your input and feedback. From today forward, I commit to being forthcoming with all information so we can be a successful team on this project. I'm asking for a second chance to do right by you. This schedule here is the schedule we have with our client, the one that I hadn't shown you guys, that shows us finishing in *June*, not May."

Roberto and Bobby exchanged a look.

Roberto frowned. "Sam, I appreciate what you're saying," he interrupted, "but if you think a couple of cold mugs of beer and some cheese nachos will make us trust you and magically help us be a stronger team, well, I'm sorry to tell you it just doesn't work that way."

Sam sighed. "I get it, guys. I understand. I should have shared all the information up front so that you guys could have been a part of planning and executing the work. That's the way it should be. Would you guys be willing to level-set and start fresh with helping me create a new schedule to finish this project? This is something I should have asked for in the first place."

The guys looked around at each other, waiting to see who would be the first to speak up.

Bobby broke the silence. "Sam, I'm not quite sure what you've got in mind, but if you're willing to really listen to us and let us be a part of creating the schedule with you, then I'm in."

Relieved, Sam grinned. "Thank you, Bobby, that's…"

"But I'll warn you," Bobby cut in, "I've done a lot of these jobs, and we're running out of time. June is going to be tough to hit. I hope you're prepared for some news you may not want to hear. If we figure out a way to get there and it's not your plan, are you going to be able to accept that?"

Sam was surprised where the conversation had headed. He was also thankful that the guys hadn't walked out.

"Deal," he said, arm outstretched. As they shook hands, Sam looked at the rest of the foremen and each agreed to be on board.

The men shared one more round. As they left the bar to start the weekend, Sam told everyone they were going to spend time working as a team on the new project schedule on Monday, in lieu of the huddle. The guys liked the sound of that.

●●●

Sam was excited to get to work Monday morning. Over the weekend, he had purchased the same supplies that Alan had in his Big Room and had them laid out on the table in the trailer next to copies of his schedule, which he'd printed out for each foreman.

For the first hour, Sam walked each foreman at the table through differences between *push* and *pull*, the airport example, and how the pull planning process would work. A few seemed overwhelmed and had a lot of questions, but while there was some skepticism they also liked the idea of being able to set their own durations.

Sam concluded the meeting by setting the pull plan date for Friday at 9:00 a.m. He emphasized multiple times how important this meeting would be, as it would be the meeting where the team built the schedule that they would all commit to in order to finish the project. He reiterated to the trades that they needed to spend time during the week thinking of all their activities, the durations for those activities, and the hand-offs they needed for their work to start. He challenged them to bring forth any constraints that they may know of, and to invite any others in their companies that would provide value to the pull plan session.

Sam called Alan on his way home from work on Monday to share the news that he was having his first pull plan on Friday morning.

"Wonderful news, Sam," said Alan. "What did the guys think?"

"Well, I'm not sure if they knew what to think, but they're willing to give this a shot. They seem bought in to the idea of providing input on activities and durations."

"That's great. Did you get all the supplies you needed?"

"Yes, I think so," replied Sam. "I'm having a board printed to show swim lanes and activity spaces like the boards on your job. I also stocked up on markers and sticky notepads, and I have a spot on my whiteboard for constraints and parking lot items."

"Perfect," Alan said. "Sounds like you're ready."

"Well...I'm not going to lie, I'm really nervous about this one, Alan. I can't stop thinking about this being my first pull plan meeting and the milestone being *the final milestone of the project*. I'm worried I'm going to mess it up and walk out of the meeting without a plan to complete by June."

"That makes sense, Sam," Alan said reassuringly. "I want you to know that I believe in you. But would you feel more comfortable if I came to co-facilitate with you? I wouldn't mind one bit."

Sam was greatly relieved. "Wow, Alan, that would be terrific. Thank you. I'd really appreciate your help."

● ● ●

When Friday morning rolled around, Sam was ready to get things rolling. Just like Alan did the previous week, he started his pull plan meeting by setting expectations and ground rules. The turn-out to the meeting was great, which was a good sign. After answering a couple questions, Sam and Alan started passing out sticky pads and markers and told the trades they had the next forty-five minutes to fill out their activity stickies, carefully noting durations and required hand-offs.

About ten minutes in, Sam and Alan started making their way around the room checking on the guys. Some of the trades had too much detail on their cards and did not clearly identify what the hand-off would be. Sam asked them to remake their cards and to be specific as to what would release work to the next trade.

Some other trades had too little information on their card, like the painter who just had one card, where he'd written the word: *paint*. Sam asked him to add more detail, explaining that the other trades wouldn't be able to easily understand where the activity was taking place, and what activities would be following.

Alan helped the team identify which conversations should go to the parking lot and which ones were relevant to talk through to release work and create a reliable workflow. As the forty-five-minute mark approached, Sam and Alan made their way to the pull board, signaling everyone for their attention.

"OK, fellas," Sam began. "Let's start mapping this out. Now, the contractual completion date is June eighteenth...and here's a sticky note for *Building Final*, with a one-day duration, and the hand-off is *MEPF Finals*."

"Don't forget, for every card there's a card that comes before it," Alan reminded everyone. "So, for Sam to get his building final, we need you to bring up the final card for your trade and place it in your row, next to Sam's card."

Hank, Bobby, Tom, Jim, and Roberto all stood up and went to the board to place their cards.

"OK," said Sam. "Jim, in order to get your plumbing final, what is the hand-off directly before it?"

Jim thought briefly, looking at the stack of stickies in his hand. In order to get his final, he would have to have all fixtures trimmed out. He handed three cards to Sam, one for each floor.

Sam looked at the durations on Jim's cards. "Hmm, this seems long, Jim. Are these durations loaded with some fluff?"

"No, sir!" said Jim, feeling a little agitated. "I followed your guidelines, and these are the real deal durations. That's the best we can give you with breaking up my two crews on three floors."

Tom went next. Sam thought his durations were also long. When Sam quizzed Tom about it, Tom threw up his hands and said, "What do you expect? We're working on all three floors at the same time!"

Over the next hour, the trades pulled back from the completion milestone, mapping out all of the necessary activities and hand-offs that needed to be achieved. When the dust settled, the pull-plan showed the last area of two-siding drywall was to be complete on March fifth. The only problem was that it was now

March twentieth, and A+ Drywall still had a week left to be done two-siding. They were tracking behind schedule by three weeks.

Sam sat down and studied his new pull plan. He was in a bit of disbelief and feeling frustrated. After a couple of minutes, it hit him.

"More guys!" he said, rising to his feet. "You all need more guys!"

"I told you we had a problem, Sam. Do you understand how busy DFW is right now? None of us have 'more guys.' This is it, Sam," Bobby said decisively. "Why don't you ask for more time?"

"You can forget that idea, Bobby!" Sam snapped. "We committed to St. Claire's board to have this job done in June, and that's the promise we are all going to keep!"

As the two men started to posture even more, Alan intervened. "Guys, calm down. This is how the pull process works. We aren't done yet, remember? This is the part of the meeting where we look at each hand-off and see if there is a different way to solve this puzzle. Now, let's take a look at the first few hand-offs," Alan said, as he walked to the whiteboard. "Jim, you mentioned two crews, broken up between three floors, doing trim out. Is that correct?"

"That's right," Jim confirmed.

"And you think it will take six weeks, so...thirty working days to complete each floor between the two crews, right?" Jim told him that was correct. "OK. Now, what if you had all your guys working on one floor at a time. What would your duration be then?"

Jim thought for a minute. "I bet we could do it in about fifteen days, maybe a day or two quicker."

Alan thought for a moment, looking at the wall of stickies. "Who else feels like they could accelerate by working on one floor at a time?" Roberto, Hank, and Tom all agreed that they could shorten their durations, too.

Alan turned to Sam. "It seems like we have a workflow issue, not a labor issue. The way we pulled this milestone has all the guys working on all the floors at the same time. What if we work our way back from starting on the third floor, and sequence the flow so that some of the finish trades don't start on the third floor until all the MEPF trades have moved down to the second floor?"

"I'm not sure I follow," said Sam. "Are you saying that the first and second floors will be sitting empty? That doesn't sound *faster* to me..."

"True, but only empty for a small time," Bobby interjected.

"Sam, the third floor and half of the second are pretty dense," Alan pointed out, referring to the drawings in front of them. "If we can trudge through those, full force, we may be able to fly with shorter durations on the second half of the first and second floors."

"I think he's right," Hank said.

Alan smiled. "What do you think, Sam? Are you willing to give it a try?"

"Let's do it," Sam said. "Let's find out."

Over the next thirty minutes the guys pulled down a few cards, wrote a few more cards, and sequenced the workflow to show all resources working their way down from the third floor as discussed. Two hours and forty-five minutes from when they had started, they stood back and admired the planning they had put in place. The pull board showed the last of the two-siding finishing on March twenty-first. They were still a bit behind, but the team thought they had a real shot at making it up and hitting the June eighteenth date.

The guys were wiped, but before Sam dismissed them he went around the room and asked for each foreman's commitment to meet the team's new schedule. Everyone was bought in. As the guys headed back to the field, Sam stared at the pull plan boards, contemplating what would be the best way to capture the information to distribute to the team.

Alan put his hand on Sam's shoulder. "You guys did great work today."

"Thanks, Alan," Sam said, still struggling to figure out how to document the meeting they just had. "Alan, back at your trailer you mentioned something about this being just a part of some type of system..."

"Yes, it's called the Last Planner System."

"Yeah, that's it! Does that Last Planner System say anything about the best way to document and share these pull plan commitments, so we don't lose track?"

"I was wondering when you were going to ask me about that," Alan said with a big smile. "I believe the enchiladas are the lunch special today at Felix's. Let's go grab a bite, and when we get back here I'll tell you more about it."

●●●

Shortly after returning to Sam's jobsite following lunch, however, Alan received a call from his client in Fort Worth. He wanted to walk the site with a board member that afternoon, and he requested Alan as their tour guide.

Alan looked at the board with all of the cards from that morning's pull plan. "I hate to leave this as unfinished business, but I need to get back to Fort Worth. We still have a lot to unpack here, and we'll need a few hours to work through it." Alan pulled up his calendar on his phone. "Let's get our ducks in a row tomorrow, and I can come back here Wednesday morning. Does that work for you?"

"Sure," said Sam. "Is there anything we can do in the meantime?"

Alan thought for a moment. "Yes. How about you and Gene start entering the commitments and durations for the milestone we just pulled back into our master schedule? We'll see where it gets us, and we can pick up from there when I come back."

Chapter Six

The Last Planner System®

The egg timer signaled the end of Wednesday's daily huddle, and Alan's truck pulled into the parking lot just as the men were exiting the trailer. Sam was eager to get back into the schedule, and he stepped outside to greet him.

"Are you ready to get to work?" Alan asked with a smile.

"I was about to ask you the same question!" Sam joked. "Gene and I are all set up in the conference room."

Alan laughed. "Great! I'm going to make a quick call and get a cup of coffee, and then I'll meet you in there."

After Alan hung up from his call, he ran into Bobby near the coffeemaker, who was predictably haunting the scattered remains of the donuts as he finished up some paperwork.

"Hey, Alan!" Bobby greeted him cheerfully. He quickly brushed the crumbs from his shirt as he rose to shake Alan's hand. "To what do I owe the pleasure of seeing you this morning? Seems like I've been running into you a lot lately."

Alan liked Bobby and was genuinely pleased to see him. "Hey, it's good to see you, too, Bobby!" he said, shaking his hand. "I'm here to meet with Sam and Gene to go over the Last Planner System."

"The last one? How many planner systems are there?" Bobby asked, confused.

Alan couldn't help but chuckle at Bobby's unintentional joke. "Tell you what: if you think your lead man can cover the field for the next hour or so, why don't you join us and I can tell you all about it, too?"

Bobby thought for a minute. Alan Phillips's reputation in the business was the gold standard from a trade partner's perspective. He was the kind of superintendent that understood the trades and what it took to make them successful. Whatever this *planner thing* was, he felt sure it was worth his time.

"You bet," Bobby agreed. "I'm always up to learn something new."

"I like that attitude!" Alan clapped Bobby's shoulder. "Let's go!"

●●●

"Gentlemen," Alan announced grandly, as he walked into the conference room, "I have brought you a *last planner* to participate in today's discussion!"

Bobby, biting into a fresh donut as he followed Alan, froze in his tracks.

"Why, because he's always *the last one done?*" Gene teased playfully.

"Very funny, pencil neck!" Bobby retorted with his mouth full.

"All right," Alan laughed. "We have a lot to cover, but I'll make it as quick as I can." Alan took another sip of his coffee and set it on the table.

"The Last Planner System actually started in the eighties, with formal development in the nineties, so what I'm saying is that this stuff is not new. Two guys, Glenn Ballard and Greg Howell, were the pioneers; they did the research that developed it, and Glenn wrote a thesis in 2000, called *The Last Planner System of Production Control*. It spells out the nuts and bolts, but if you're not the thesis-reading type, today you'll get the CliffsNotes version from me."

"That works for me," Sam quipped. "I'm smack in the middle of a thesis and can't start another."

Gene laughed. "Seriously, though, these guys sound like some smart dudes."

"Yeah, they were definitely ahead of their time," continued Alan. "They laid out the foundation of a production control process that's specific to construction. Then, in 1997, they joined together to form the Lean Construction Institute, where they've worked to transform the industry by promoting and facilitating Lean adoption. They provide education, resources, and best practices for all of us."

"Geez, what rock have I been living under?" Sam mused. "I've never even heard of it."

"Well, maybe you haven't, but a lot a people have, and it's a shame that this approach isn't the standard for our industry. But I promise you, one day it will be, because our current state is broken. So, I tell you all of that to tell you this: Bobby here is the *last planner*, because the project trade partner foremen are the people ultimately responsible for getting the work done through planning and efficient execution."

"Yeah, the buck stops here!" Bobby crowed.

"It's true!" Alan affirmed. "Sam, walk me through how you built your master schedule for this project."

"Well, Gene and I spent a couple of days studying the drawings and specs and building out the Gantt schedule, based on what we saw and on our previous experience, for how long we thought it would take for the trades to complete the tasks."

Alan nodded. "Right. And our clients expect that. As a construction management firm, we are expected to have this knowledge to let our clients and architects know how long a project should take. But as we learned last week, when talking about *push* versus *pull*, this schedule is a *push schedule*; it's a forecast based off of what we think we know at the early phase of the project life-cycle."

"Why, whatever do you mean, Alan?" Sam asked, with feigned surprise. "Gene's schedules are perfect; all activities start on Mondays and finish on Fridays."

"Are you tired of him?" Gene asked Bobby, gesturing towards Sam. "I'm tired of him."

"We should have brought Elmo in here," Bobby laughed.

"And, as we also learned last week," Alan continued, sliding his arm around Bobby's shoulder, "we need the expertise and participation of these last planners to help us plan, sequence, commit, and ultimately validate the project schedule."

Sam nodded. "Joking aside, everything you've said makes sense. I get it."

Alan smiled. "OK, grab a seat and take some notes. I'm going to walk you through it."

The men got settled at the table as Alan began. "The first part of the Last Planner System is to *create the master schedule* and to *set the milestones*. As Sam mentioned, this was your pretty schedule that started Monday and ended on Friday." Alan winked at Gene. "This is called Master Scheduling.

"The second part of the Last Planner System is what we did on Monday. We had a reverse phase schedule session, or a pull plan, where we specified hand-offs, allowed an environment of collaboration between the last planners, and identified flow. All of this allowed the team to validate the milestones we pulled in from the master schedule. This is called Phase Scheduling."

Alan paused for a moment. "Sam, did you input the commitments and the durations from the pull plan session into the master schedule?"

Sam nodded as Gene began to open the file on his laptop. "We wrapped that up yesterday afternoon."

"Great. Inputting the milestone commitments from the pull plan back into your master schedule is the final check in Phase Scheduling. What we are going to learn about now is something called Lookahead Planning and the Weekly Work Plan."

Alan turned to Bobby. "When it comes to the schedule, what are you used to seeing on this project and others, from a trade's perspective?"

Bobby scratched his chin. "If we're lucky, we usually see some sort of Gantt chart updated once a month or so. To be honest, they are kind of hard to read and follow along to see where we are in the job."

Gene nodded. "That's pretty accurate."

"Well, that's not how the Last Planner System works," Alan explained. "In the Phase Scheduling portion of the system, the construction manager/general contractor will issue a six-week look-ahead to the team, based on the previously-completed milestone pull plan. This is where you are in the process right now."

"OK, here we go," said Gene, turning his screen so everyone could see.

"Thanks," said Alan. "Now, you have a couple of options here, Sam. If you or Gene are good with the scheduling software, you can easily print a six-week snapshot straight from the program. If the scheduling program makes you feel uneasy, you can easily pull the six-week information from the master schedule and input it into a simple Gantt spreadsheet. Sometimes this is a bit easier for people who are not as familiar with the scheduling software."

"Makes sense," Sam agreed.

"As a part of the look-ahead plan, or six-week look-ahead, I like to show *who is responsible* for each line item of work and *identify constraints* that still exist that could delay upcoming workflow,"

Alan explained. "It's important that you issue a six-week look-ahead to the last planners every week. I prefer Fridays, because that allows the team to see the road-map and plan out their work for the coming week.

"So, to summarize: the third part of the Last Planner System is initiated once the phase or pull schedule has been completed and updated back in the master schedule. We then issue a six-week look-ahead every week which identifies make-ready activities, shows potential constraints that need to be buffered or removed, clearly sets responsibilities and commitments for trade partners, and helps last planners allocate resources. This is called Lookahead Planning."

Alan surveyed the group. "I know this is a lot. Is everyone following so far?"

Bobby was the first to speak. "I like what I'm hearing, Alan. What's great about the pull plan, or the phase scheduling portion, is that I get to put my fate in my own hands, so-to-speak. Making a commitment about what we think we can do is much better than being told what we can or can't do. We see that a lot on my side of the business. The look-ahead planning part makes sense, too; an updated six-week schedule every week would be nice to help keep people on track. But my question is: what happens when things go *off track*?"

"Tell me what you mean by 'off track'?" Alan pressed.

"Like a missed inspection, or materials not delivered on time, or a coordination issue that needs to be solved. Those things eat up schedule. The problem is the project superintendent—no offense,

Sam—never seems to account for that when the next version of the schedule comes out. It's like we're supposed to just magically make it up with more men or more overtime or whatever."

Sam thought about the way he'd normally react to schedule setbacks and felt a pang of guilt.

"It almost seems like we need to do a pull plan every week to make sure the project superintendent is up-to-date on how some of these constraints are affecting the workflow in the field, which ultimately could affect the commitment we made."

Alan nodded. "That's a great observation. The bad news is that we probably don't have time to have a pull plan every week. The good news is, the Last Planner System has accounted for this in something called Weekly Work Plans. The Weekly Work Plan is one of the most important roles for a last planner. The last planner's Weekly Work Plan is essentially a commitment plan. Last planners must commit only to work that can be done."

"But...*how?*" Bobby asked.

"By the last planners also having a say in the Weekly Work Plan," Alan answered. "The last planners had their first say while buying into the schedule, when they made commitments to each other at the pull plan. As we just learned, this information made its way into the first six-week look-ahead distributed by the project superintendent. But, as you correctly pointed out, Bobby, things change in the field. Where the trades help keep the project on track is by filling out a three-week work plan that breaks down the information from the six-week schedule into smaller chunks of work, and helps the project superintendent identify if the team is still on track before he updates and distributes the six-week look-ahead the following week."

"Let me make sure I have this," Sam began. "Gene and I issue the first six-week schedule after our initial milestone pull plan session. Then, before we issue the next six-week look-ahead the following week, we ask the trades to fill out a three-week work plan that breaks down their scope into smaller activities..."

"That's right," Alan encouraged.

"...and we're supposed to use that information to build our next six-week look-ahead schedule," concluded Gene.

"Yes, that's it!" Alan exclaimed.

"Can you give us an example?" Sam asked.

"Of course," Alan replied. "Gene, let's take a look at the six-week schedule you have pulled up on your screen, and use A+ Drywall as our example."

"OK," said Gene, pointing to his monitor. "On this six-week look-ahead, derived from the commitments made in the pull plan, we show tape, bed, and first coat on the third floor taking place during weeks one, two, and three. Bobby, your ceiling grid is starting on week two, and continuing through weeks three and four. Light fixtures show to be installing on week three and continuing on through weeks four and five."

"From a high level, would you all agree this makes sense?" Alan quizzed. The men exchanged looks and nodded.

"But, as Bobby explained earlier, in the construction business things can go off track in a hurry," Alan suggested. "So, let's say that the ductwork insulators got behind in certain areas of the third floor where there are large portions of ductwork and high ceiling heights, which made insulating more difficult and time-consuming. Now, Sam, how would this information typically make its way back to you?"

"Usually, a dogfight in the field," Sam needled, nudging Bobby with his elbow. "But, more recently, it would come up at our daily huddle."

"That's right, I would show the areas where I'm shut down on the visual communication plans."

"Great," Alan continued, "but to your point from earlier, it's going to take time to get that ductwork insulated. That's the point of the three-week look-ahead: we're trying to catch these constraints *before they reveal themselves during the work week*, so we can *make alternate recovery plans prior to scheduling work*. That way, the project can achieve the most reliable workflow possible."

"I get it!" Gene blurted, hopping out of his seat. "If we received a Weekly Work Plan from the last planners each week showing potential constraints to the flow of work, like in this example with the uninsulated ductwork, we could look for ways on our six-week look-ahead to re-sequence the painter to hit areas that allow ceiling grid to continue being installed until the ductwork insulation is compete. This way, no time is lost!"

"BINGO!" Alan cheered.

Sam frowned. "I'm not sure I see the big picture, Alan. I agree that a three-week look-ahead from each trade could alleviate constraints and help with a more accurate six-week look-ahead. But it seems like each trade filling out a schedule and then sending them back to me to review and enter into a six-week format every week is *a lot of time* spent on *a lot of paperwork*."

"Yeah," Gene reluctantly agreed, sliding back into his chair. "This does seem like a lot of work."

"I hear you," reassured Alan. "I struggled with what you're describing. So, a few years ago I went over to the reprographics shop and asked if they could print out a blank three-week look-ahead schedule on an oversized dry erase laminate board."

"Hey, I think I remember seeing that board in your Big Room!" Sam noted.

Alan nodded. "Yep! In the spirit of visual communication, why deal with all that paperwork that's not out in the open? On Friday mornings, the last planners come into the big room in our trailer and fill out their activities, the duration, how many men are working, and any constraints not allowing them to start or complete activities. Then, I review throughout the day, ask questions to the last planners, and then update my six-week schedule and launch it out to the team before heading home for the weekend. Then we review this board at the daily huddle each day."

"And this works?" Sam challenged. "It really WORKS?"

"It works very well," Alan assured. "You have to keep at it until it does, but it does work."

The men were impressed.

"Alan! You've been holding out on us. How come you didn't tell us all of this back when you first told me about daily huddles?" Sam implored.

"Patience, young grasshopper!" Alan laughed. "You have to crawl before you can walk, right? It was important that you developed a strong foundation of tools and processes as you progressed in your journey.

"OK," Alan continued. "To summarize: the fourth part of the Last Planner System is having each last planner create a weekly work assignment—for example, a three-week look-ahead schedule— which conveys reliable promises, identifies constraints, and shores up the project workflow, which feeds back up into the six-week schedule for reliable look-ahead planning. This is called Weekly Work Planning."

Alan paused, looking like he wanted to say more. The guys waited, ready to take more notes.

"There is another step to part four...but I don't want us to get ahead of ourselves today. You boys have a lot of work to do to get this implemented in a way that will get this project back on track. Issue your six-week look-ahead today and get moving on getting a three-week look-ahead board hung and populated by next Friday. Then, over the next few weeks, you'll be implementing the following tools at the huddle: the three-week look-ahead board, the constraint board, the visual communication boards, and the six-week look-ahead schedule. Oh, and here's a tip: I always post my six-week look-ahead right next to my three-week look-ahead board as a 'cheat sheet' for the last planners."

Sam nodded and then grinned at Gene, who let out a big sigh and then returned Sam's smile.

At that moment, Kate entered the job trailer for her weekly walk with Sam. "Hi, Sam, sorry to interrupt!"

"You're not interrupting at all! Your timing is perfect." Sam introduced Kate to the team, and then turned to Alan and shook his hand. "Thank you, Alan. You've been so helpful. We will get moving on this ASAP."

Bobby shook Alan's hand, too. "I really appreciate you including me in this!"

"Absolutely!" Alan replied. "I'm glad you could be here."

Sam grabbed his notepad and led Kate out into the field. He felt ready to get this process moving.

● ● ●

Over the next week, Sam and Gene did everything Alan recommended. The trades were working off an updated six-week look-ahead based on the pull, and they had a nearby reprographics shop print out an oversized three-week look-ahead board. Sam and Bobby also taught the other foremen—the last planners, as Bobby liked to refer to them now—about how the Last Planner System worked and the important role the trades had in it. Roberto liked the fact that *he* was being asked for his input instead of *his office*, as they tended to tell the construction manager/general contractor what they *wanted* to hear, not what they *needed* to hear. Hank felt like it was really built for the guys in the field, and Jim liked that about it as well.

All week, Sam had been reminding everyone that, after Friday's huddle, he wanted each last planner to update the next three weeks of their work activities on the new board. When Friday came around, Bobby went first. He started at the top row and worked his way down. Next, he used his marker to fill in his planned work in the column designated for activities, and he indicated the number of men he had working on each activity in the work week column. But when it was time for him to fill in the constraints to the activities in the constraint column, Bobby stalled.

"Hey, Sam, what is the difference between the constraints on this board and the constraint board?"

"I'm glad you asked that," Sam began. "The constraints we identify here on the three-week look-ahead board are budding impacts that, if not properly addressed, could negatively affect the activities listed on the three-week look-ahead. The constraints that get put on the constraint board, however, come from the morning huddles and are imminent threats to our workflow if we don't have a sense of urgency about resolving them."

Bobby still looked confused. Sam tried again. "OK, here's another way to think about it. It's almost like torpedo radar. You may notice that I have a constraint column in the six-week look-ahead I send out. That is the first sign that a torpedo—or, in this case, a constraint—has hit our radar. When it shows up on your three-week look-ahead, it's closer to hitting its target. By the time it hits the constraint board in the huddle, we've been hit dead on."

Bobby nodded and told Sam that was a helpful analogy for him. He completed his constraints for the three-week look-ahead, and then he and Sam reviewed what he'd written.

Sam scratched his head. "Bobby, how many men do you have onsite?"

"Twelve."

"But look at the four tasks you wrote down. If you add up the number of guys for each day, it totals to sixteen."

"Well," Bobby began, "a few of the guys we have installing grid can also swing doors. I'm not sure which day the doors will come in, so I showed those guys in both columns."

"I understand," said Sam, "but let's try to define the activities the best we can with your resources over the upcoming three weeks."

Bobby adjusted the manpower and days on the board. "How do I look?"

"This looks good, Bobby! If you can get this kind of production over the next three weeks, we may actually pick up some time."

An hour later Tom came into the room, studied what Bobby had written, and then followed suit by filling in his team's activities. Sam studied the board when Tom was finished. "This looks good, Tom, but your activities are a little vague. You show three weeks of turning down heads on the third floor, but where are you starting and where are you finishing?" Tom realized what he'd missed and went back to fill in Areas A, B, and C, next to his various activities. Sam checked his six-week look-ahead and gave Tom a pat on the back.

This continued throughout the day, and ultimately concluded with Roberto. Sam studied what Roberto had written and then looked back to the six-week look-ahead. "Hey, Roberto, I'm not trying to pick on you, but looking at this six-week look-ahead you seem to be a bit long with the light fixture install on the third floor. Don't forget these were your dates from the pull plan that we plugged in."

"I know," Roberto admitted unhappily. "Since the pull, one of my lead electricians got pulled off to another job—his replacement is good, but he doesn't have the knowledge and job history my other electrician did. I worry it's going to take him a bit longer to install."

"How about working ten-hour days?" Sam suggested.

Roberto wanted to avoid this, though. "How about this...I'll jump in at the beginning to help my guys and see if we can stay on track. If not, we'll work longer."

Sam was satisfied with that answer and smiled. "Sounds like a deal!" But Roberto still looked sheepish. "Everything else OK?"

Roberto cleared his throat. "Sam, the light fixtures on this job had a ten-week lead time. We are on week twelve, and they still haven't shipped. I've been told that they will air freight quick-ship this weekend, which should allow us to start Wednesday as planned, but I don't have the warm fuzzies."

Sam was surprised. "Wow. How come you didn't tell us when they didn't ship out a few weeks ago?"

"I'm sorry. My office kept telling me they were coming, and I knew we weren't installing for a few weeks. I didn't want to make a mountain out of a molehill—but, looking back, I probably should have been up front with you sooner," Roberto reluctantly explained.

"OK, go ahead and add it to the constraint column on the three-week look-ahead board, and let me know as soon as you hear something."

Roberto added the constraint to the board and headed back to the field. Sam reviewed the three-week look-ahead board and liked what he saw. While his wall didn't look quite like Alan's, he had a six-week schedule posted, a three-week look-ahead board that tracked upcoming milestones, work activities, and manpower. He also had his constraint board and his laminated floor plans. He felt like he had a perfect dashboard to manage his project, and he smiled at the hard work and progress that all of these tools represented.

Sam made his rounds, finished his daily report, and closed the job for the weekend. With the overall project still behind the eight ball, it was definitely going to be a rush to the finish, but he felt more prepared than he ever had.

Sam's weekend was a whirlwind. He spent Saturday morning at the grocery store picking up cases of water, soft drinks, and a few catering trays, followed by a stop at the party store for balloons and streamers. His mom and Jen's were both at the house, cooking, cleaning, putting the finishing touches on a large sheet cake, and transforming the dining and living rooms into a baby shower wonderland while Jen spent time with her feet up at a nearby spa with two of her sisters. At 1:00 p.m., the house was a busy mix of noise and activity with the addition of three grandmas, Jen's other two sisters, three sisters-in-law, Elsie, a dozen or so of Jen's coworkers and assorted friends, and a blur of squealing nieces and nephews.

Sam retreated to the beer fridge in the garage with his brother, Jen's dad and brothers, Alan, and a few random husbands who'd tagged along with their wives. They admired Sam's "new" riding mower, which he'd recently bought used from a neighbor, vigorously debated whether the Cowboys' quarterback was a great Super Bowl quarterback or just a game manager, and strategized over the merits of live bait versus various fishing lures for his and Alan's planned trip to Lake Texoma to catch striper the following weekend. As much fun as he was having, Sam couldn't help but miss his dad and Andrew.

After the last of their guests had finally left, Sam moved furniture back where it belonged, vacuumed, and pitched in with the clean-up. (Jen complained there was too much leftover cake, so he was happy to help out as much as he could there, too, cutting off large bites every time he passed through the kitchen.) By the time they went to bed that night, he was exhausted.

He made it to the job Monday morning just in time to get the coffee pot on and fire up his laptop before the trades started to make their way into the trailer. Sam noticed they had gathered around the three-week look-ahead board and were pointing at different items as they talked amongst themselves. They seemed to be impressed with their work now that it was completely filled in.

"Good morning, last planners!" Sam began. "All right, remember there is nothing new about how we are doing the huddles. Each one of you will answer the same questions as always: what you are working on, where you are working, how many men are working, and what your constraints or needs are. I'd also like to know what material deliveries you have coming up." Sam turned on the egg timer and the guys got started.

Bobby went first. He started at the three-work board, explaining to everyone that he had three crews of four men installing grid and doors on the third floor. Then he circled the areas where his men would be working on the laminated floor plans. "We're on track with the six-week look-ahead. I don't have any constraints, and the only delivery we have is on Friday, which'll be the ceiling tile for Area A."

The rest of the trades followed suit. When Roberto got through where his men were going to be working, he brought up to the entire team that he had a potential constraint of the third-floor light fixtures being late and showed where he'd documented this on the three-work board.

Sam then read through all the constraints on the constraint board while erasing ones that had been resolved and confirming due dates with the responsible trades for the ones that were still open. Before closing the meeting, Sam went around the room with each trade to confirm that there was no new business or constraints that weren't previously discussed, and that everyone was on board with what needed to be completed that day. The men looked around the room and nodded. The meeting was adjourned with a few men sticking around to talk about a handful of items that did not concern everyone.

After everyone had left, Sam called Gene to make sure he was aware of the light fixture issue on the third floor. "I heard, and I'm on it!" he confirmed. "We have a call tomorrow afternoon with B&B and their supply house. I'll let you know what I find out."

Tuesday morning's huddle went well, but Sam noticed halfway through that some of the trade partners still seemed to direct all conversation directly to him even when talking about another trade. Sam called a time out and reminded the guys that this meeting was their opportunity to communicate and solve issues with the person that had the most influence and opportunity to fix their issue and their constraints.

Later that afternoon, Sam got a call from Gene with news about the light fixtures.

"OK, so the fixtures are en route..." Gene began.

"That's great!" Sam gushed, relieved.

"...BUT," Gene emphasized, "They won't be onsite until Friday."

Sam thanked Gene and hung up. Just then, the trailer door swung open and Roberto stepped inside, and he saw Sam's expression.

"You've heard?" he guessed.

"Yes, Gene just told me the news." Sam walked up to the six-week look-ahead board on the wall. "Roberto, this is going to put you behind two days. What are our options?"

"I'm going to pull some strings and get my lead foreman back from the job he's on for both Friday and Saturday. I'll put my tool belt on to help, also. I think we can make it up."

"Man, that would be awesome," Sam said, gratefully. "I appreciate you trying to make that happen."

After Roberto went back into the field, Sam felt encouraged. There was a time earlier in the project that there would have been no way Roberto would have been so eager to put his tools back on to make sure his commitment to the team was completed.

The Last Planner System seemed like it would be hard to implement and maintain, but the benefits were freeing up so much of Sam's time to focus on staying at 10,000 feet, he really wished he could have started his project this way.

The team seemed to be gaining good ground, and after the huddle on Friday Sam went up to the board and snapped a photo with his cellphone. Alan had told him it would be a good idea to photograph and print the previous week's board and post it to the wall, as well as distribute it to the last planners' project managers, to provide awareness of how the team did that week and help to make sure the trades' offices were in alignment with the commitments that were being made in the field.

Before Sam wiped down the boards for the trades to begin populating the upcoming week, he compared what *should have been done* to what his updated six-week look-ahead showed *would be done*. He realized that a few of the trades' items did not fully complete, which would cause them to slip a day or two into the upcoming week. Sam thought something seemed incomplete with the Last Planner System, and he remembered Alan mentioning some final part to the entire thing. He decided to give him a quick call.

"Howdy, stranger!" Alan said, happy to hear from Sam. "Ready for tomorrow?"

Sam drew a blank.

"Don't tell me you forgot about striper fishing at Lake Texoma!" Alan said with a laugh. "That baby will be here before you know it and you won't have many opportunities to wet a line."

Sam smiled. "Heck no, I didn't forget it! In fact, I picked up some fresh swim baits last night. I will be packed and ready at 5:00 a.m. sharp. Sorry, I was just preoccupied."

"Well, if you weren't calling to discuss the trophy striper I'm going to catch this weekend, what's up?"

Sam laughed. "I was calling to tell you that my guys are crushing it with the three-week look-ahead and are totally bought into the Last Planner System process."

"You just made my week," Alan said, genuinely pleased. "Making up any time?"

"I think we just may be. Had a bit of a hiccup with some light fixtures, but we're pushing ahead of schedule in some other areas. I do think I have an idea, though, that could make the three-week look-ahead better..."

"Oh, really? I'm curious to hear your thoughts."

"Well, it's just that we wrapped up our week, and I was thinking that if we had some type of score card or something, some way of tracking how we did on each of the commitments, it may help us be more productive," Sam explained. "Also, did I remember you saying something about a final piece to the whole Last Planner System?"

"You're right," Alan began. "I haven't shared the one final piece of the Last Planner System with you and it is one of the most important. I didn't want to give you more to bite off than you could chew, but you guys are doing great. The last component of the system, and the one you learn the most from, is something called Percent Plan Complete, or just PPC for short."

"Percent Plan Complete," Sam repeated, unfamiliar with the terminology.

"We have a two-hour drive tomorrow morning up to the lake. If you don't mind talking shop, I can fill you in with the details when we are on the road."

"It beats listening to you sing along to the radio," Sam joked.

"Hey, I make no promises there!"

Sam hung up and smiled. He was really looking forward to his weekend with Alan. It was hard to believe that in just two more months this building would be done, and he would be a dad.

Chapter Seven

Percent Plan Complete

It was still dark at 5:00 a.m. on Saturday morning as Alan turned onto Sam's street. He was itching to get to the lake, and he wondered if Sam was as excited for the day as he was. When his headlights found Sam at the end of his driveway, waiting by his cooler with a fishing rod in one hand and a Thermos of hot coffee in the other, he laughed out loud.

"Morning, sunshine!" Alan greeted Sam as he opened the door. "Ready to thump these stripers today?"

"You bet," Sam answered. "They won't know what hit 'em!"

The men chatted comfortably as they cruised to the highway and started heading north to Lake Texoma. As they watched the sky start to pink up, their conversation turned from striper fishing, to Cowboys football, to newborn babies.

"Well, you sure cleaned up at the baby shower! I know you two decided to let the gender be a surprise, but have you picked out any names yet?" Alan asked.

Sam nodded as he unscrewed the cap from his Thermos. "I think we've landed on a few we like, but Jen and I still go back and forth because *one of us* keeps changing *her* mind."

"Yeah, I know a little bit about how that works!" Alan chuckled. "Just make sure it's not one of those weird, newfangled names that I always hear when my grandkids' friends come by."

"Are you trying to tell me you don't like the name Alphabet? Or Juggernaut?!" Sam implored.

"OK, Alphabet is a hard NO," Alan answered with mock seriousness. "But *Juggernaut*? Now you've got me reevaluating things."

"I know, it's awesome," joked Sam. "And it works for a boy OR a girl."

"Well, I hadn't thought about it for a *boy's* name, but yeah, I think you're right!"

From there, the conversation headed towards Alan's new smoker, covered a fussy timing belt issue on Sam's mower, and then meandered to their respective projects at work.

"Alan, all of this stuff you've been teaching me...how long have you been into this and implementing it at ProCon Builders?"

"Lean Construction?" Alan thought for a minute. "I reckon it's been a little over five years."

Sam was surprised. "Only five years? Wow, I would have thought it was a lot longer than that. From what I've been told by other superintendents, you've never had a job that lost money or finished late. Why would you change the way you run work five years ago if what you did before that obviously worked so well?"

"Is that what they say?" Alan asked, laughing. "Well, it's true that most of my projects have been winners; however, over time I started noticing that the industry was changing. What it took to get jobs to the finish line was starting to require more work and create more stress."

"Really? What changed?"

Alan whistled. "Short answer? *Everything.* The long answer starts with construction documents. Early in my career, the design teams had more time to put together a package of drawings. Architects drew each detail by hand, which required more thought and planning up-front. But today, the construction documents aren't what they used to be—and that's not a dig at our architect partners. It's the demand for their services, and a need for everything to happen faster, which leads to our reliance on technology—just the way our industry has evolved.

"But it's not just that. The craftsmen aren't what they once were, either. Growing up, master carpenters were like artists. Being an ironworker or a mason was something to aspire to. A lot of kids were interested in getting into the trades when they finished high school, but not anymore. For some reason, the idea of working with your hands has a negative connotation in our society today, and all the emphasis is on going to college. Don't get me wrong, there's nothing wrong with college. Elsie was an educator for thirty years, and she pushed so many students to achieve a good education, perhaps so they could get into college. But I think we do kids a disservice when we don't let them see that they can build a good career and make good money in the construction industry.

"Anyway, the point here is that, as a consequence, there aren't enough craftsmen to go around, and the craftsmen that we do have just don't know the documents like they used to. They're spread too thin or pulled in too late. You know, nowadays, it is not a surprise if a foreman comes to your job for the first time and they haven't looked at the documents yet. Again, like with our designer friends, this is not the trade partner's fault. This is the reality of the world our trade partners live in based on the current industry demand."

Sam was blown away. He hadn't known the construction industry to be any different from the way it was today, but Alan had a distinctly different view.

"But you asked what changed *for me*, and the answer is that a little over five years ago I finished the hardest project of my career to that point. And it shouldn't have been that way, but long story short is we made it by the skin of our teeth. It wiped me out and had me feeling pretty low about the current state of affairs in our business. I needed a break, so Elsie and I loaded up the fifth wheel and headed for the mountains of Montana, close to where I spent a lot of time growing up as a child. We set up our campsite, and I realized I hadn't packed enough firewood for the trip, so I needed to go out and secure some more to get us through the first few nights.

"As I got the hatchet out of the storage bin in the back of the camper, I ran my thumb across the blade, and noticed that it had been a while since I sharpened the blade of my camping hatchet. I struggled for close to an hour, chopping away at dead limbs, and when I got back to the campsite Elsie joked and reminded me that I'm not as young as I used to be, owing to the fact I looked pretty worn out for such a small stash of firewood. Later that evening, after Elsie had gone to bed, I was enjoying the last of the fire and my mind wandered to something I learned from my father..."

Alan liked to talk and started to feel like he was chattering away too much. "Sam, sorry to bend your ear so much this morning. Do you mind if I tell you a story that will help explain the reason for the shift in how I view work?"

Sam, who'd always been captivated by Alan's storytelling, had just been thinking how much this reminded him of other road trips with Alan when he was a kid. Alan was full of stories and had a great way of telling them—even if you'd heard them before, you still wanted him to tell them again. Sam urged him to go on.

"It was early summer, going into my senior year of high school, and I was confident—some may say cocky—in my physical abilities as a young man. After breakfast early one Saturday morning, my old man asked me to clean the horse stalls, put down fresh bedding, and do a few other chores I loathed while he went out to down a handful of mature trees to get the lumber he needed for a new loafing shed.

"Being the cavalier young man that I was, I joked and asked if his back was up to the task. My dad lowered his chin, raised his eyebrows, and looked down at me over the top of his glasses like I was a small curiosity.

"'Don't think your old man still has it in him, huh?' he asked me, impassively.

"I smiled in my haughty way and suggested maybe he should take care of the stalls and leave the tree cutting to me." Alan chuckled at the memory.

"So, my dad says, 'I tell you what, son. Why don't you grab your axe, and I'll grab my axe, and we'll see who can drop the most trees before the lunch bell rings. Fella with the most downed trees doesn't have to clean the stalls.'

"My mouth moved a lot faster than my brain did back then, and I wanted to show my old man just how good I was. So, I popped up quick from the breakfast table and we shook on it. I grabbed my axe without so much as a backwards glance or another thought in my head, and we took our positions in the forest and commenced to chopping. I was confident with every swing I took and thought to myself, *There is no way my old man is beating me today.*

"What gave an even bigger boost to my confidence, like I needed it, was I could hear my father at work a couple hundred yards away from me, and every hour or so his axe would go silent for five or ten minutes. I just knew I had him licked, as I believed he was running out of gas, so when he was at rest I doubled my effort. I pushed myself twice as hard and gave it everything I had. As the mid-day sun started to take its place in the sky, I was dripping with sweat and pretty much useless, but I had no doubt that I'd bested my father that day.

"Satisfied with myself, I made my way back to where we parted to find him waiting for me with a certain kind of smile on his face. Over the next hour we walked together and counted the trees we'd both cut down; I couldn't believe it—the old man annihilated me. It wasn't even close, almost two to one.

"I felt like my eyes were lying to me—and if I'm honest, I was pretty raw about it, as that was a lofty perch he'd pushed me from." Sam laughed at this, and Alan grinned.

"I asked him, 'How did you do it? I heard you sucking wind at the end of every hour!'

"He said, 'You're right, I was tired, but what you heard was not me just taking a breather. I was also sharpening my axe, son.' Already knowing the answer, he asked me, 'How many times did you sharpen your axe today?'

"My face grew hot with the realization of my foolishness. I confessed that it hadn't occurred to me to sharpen my axe all morning; my mind was singularly fixated on beating him at chopping wood.

"'And how many times did you break to renew yourself?' he prodded.

"'None, sir,' I replied, miserably.

"Taking pity on me, he complimented me on how hard I'd worked. But then he explained that one of us worked *harder* and the other worked *smarter*—and that smart working beats hard working any day of the week. He taught me that I didn't need to wear myself out to win; I needed to keep my blade sharp and my body rested to preserve my stamina."

Alan was quietly reflective for a moment. Then he added, "The old man was right, and he usually was."

Sam had heard a lot of stories about Alan's dad over the years, some several times (including this one), and this was probably his favorite one. Sam noticed that these stories always seemed to end with, "The old man was right, and he usually was." It was clear to Sam how much Alan had respected and loved his dad.

Alan cleared his throat. "Anyway, his lesson came back to me as I sat around the campfire that night. Of course, I realized that I had not sharpened my camping axe, but—more importantly, over the last thirty years—I had not 'sharpened my axe' when it came to my craft. I just came in, day in and day out, and wore myself out, chopping away at the wood with a dull blade. I knew I needed to 'sharpen my blade' at work; I needed a new way to approach an industry that was changing, and maybe leaving the old guys like me behind. From that trip came my big 'ah-ha moment.'

"When I got back to Dallas, I started asking every trade partner and architect I knew if there was something they had seen or heard of that took a different approach to the way things had always been in the construction industry. And from that curiosity, I was introduced to Lean Construction. I took in everything I could find, read books, and started going to Community of Practice meetings. The more I learned, the more I liked it and the more it all made sense. Then I started to add elements of it to my jobs, and before long I could tell that I was working smarter. And the rest, as they say, is history."

Sam thanked Alan for sharing the story, and the truck was relatively quiet for the remainder of the drive to the marina. He replayed Alan's story in his mind and, as he did, he couldn't help but think about his own life and career. He wondered if he had ever really taken the time to "sharpen his blade." He felt like he had always looked to continuously improve in all of the categories that were important to him—physically, socially, spiritually. But with how much thoughtful intent? And what about his work, and his career?

Sam was still chewing on these thoughts as he boarded the fishing guide's boat to head out.

●●●

The day started a little slow with the guide using some swim baits, but after a couple of hours the guide went back to the marina with a cast net, landed three to four dozen shad, and then they switched to live bait. From that point on, they were on fire; Sam landed three ten-to-twelve-pound class stripers and Alan pulled in a half a dozen or so good striper box fish. The guys laughed, cracked jokes, and talked about old times. Sam really enjoyed the moment, not thinking about work, or becoming a new dad, as they fished.

On the drive back home, Sam got a weather alert on his phone which ended up steering the conversation back to work.

"Alan, the pull plan session and the six- and three-week look-aheads are really working great. But you have to tell me about this Percent Plan Complete thing—what is it, and how does it work?"

"Well," Alan began, "according to LCI, Percent Plan Complete measures how well the planning on a job is working. It calculates the number of promises/activities *completed* and divides that by the total number of promises/activities *made* by the last planners each week. It's a measurement that yields a percentage of commitments met."

Sam tried to process this. "That sounds complex. Can you explain how you use it in the field?"

"Sure. My Friday huddles run about five minutes longer than the others the rest of the week. After each trade has discussed what they are working on, where they are working, the crew size, and their constraints, we score our commitments for the week on Fridays."

"Commitments?" Sam pressed. "I thought the activities on the board represented production for that week."

"No, Sam, the activities that the last planners populate on the three-week look-ahead board are *commitments they are promising to the entire team that they will complete.* Percent Plan Complete is about *measuring the commitments that were met* and *understanding the root cause for commitments that were not met.* This is not production tracking."

Sam thought for a moment. "So, the goal is to hit one hundred percent of the commitments that were made each week?"

Alan laughed. "That would be great, but I warn you that PPC is not a report card and one hundred percent isn't the ultimate goal.

A higher completion percentage may not translate into a project functioning at a higher level."

This made absolutely no sense to Sam.

Alan could sense his confusion. "You may find that the trades are sandbagging and not challenging themselves. The goal is to reduce the mindset of empty promises and to try to continuously improve."

It clicked. "OK! I like the sound of that!" Sam exclaimed. "So, after the huddle on Fridays you grade each commitment for the week?"

"That's right. And it's black or white. If your electrician commits to installing all the light fixtures on the first floor by Friday and only gets ninety-five percent of the light fixtures installed, then he gets a zero percent on the PPC. Its either a one hundred or a zero."

"That seems kind of harsh, Alan."

"Remember, Sam, we are measuring *commitments* and not *productivity*. Let's say your electrical and plumbing foremen commit to getting their in-wall finals on Friday. They get ninety-five percent complete, but ultimately miss their inspection. Doesn't that affect the project schedule?"

Sam nodded.

"If we can't have reliable commitments, we can't accurately plan to have a reliable workflow."

"I hadn't thought of it that way," Sam acknowledged. "So, after you score the commitments for the week, then what?"

"Well, first we divide the activities completed against the commitments made to establish the PPC percentage. But the real magic happens when you look at the activities that were missed and dig into the root cause for why the commitment wasn't made. I track the following root causes for work not complete:

- Weather
- Manpower
- Machinery
- Design
- Make-ready needs
- Materials
- Poor scheduling."

Fascinated, Sam had begun taking notes on the back of an empty Whataburger bag. "Do you keep track per trade for scoring, or for the overall team?"

"I used to do it by trade," Alan admitted, "but the data can be skewed when looking at make-ready needs. If a drywall trade is ready with adequate manpower and materials to perform their commitment but can't start because a plumbing inspection is missed, their commitment will also be missed, and it is not really their fault. That's why now I only track it as a team metric."

"Got it. So, what do you do with the metrics? I mean, once you score the Percent Plan Complete and capture the root causes for work not complete, then what?"

"Well, the beauty of the system is what I do *before* I capture the root cause for work not being complete. Before I started doing daily huddles and had a three-week look-ahead board, I would have a hunch that a trade partner was getting behind, but by the time I knew for certain there was an issue it was often too late without significant cost and heartburn. I needed a system to know the train was about to come off the tracks *before* it happened.

"For example, let's say a drywall crew commits to having the second floor two-sided by Friday. And, let's say they show on the three-week look-ahead board that it will take them eight men per day to get there. On Monday, if they only have four men, and on Tuesday they only have five, my 'spider senses' are activated, as my grandkids would say."

Sam and Alan laughed at this.

"Something's going amiss, right?" Alan continued. "So, I have a conversation and remind that trade partner it's not just about hitting the activity by Friday; it's about releasing the work behind him as committed. If he is supposed to complete twenty percent of the work on the second floor per day and decides to slam all of it in the last day, that does not allow the tape and bed crews behind him to meet their commitments as promised."

"You're right," Sam agreed. "That makes sense."

"Now, you asked me what I do with the metrics created from PPC. Well, for starters I utilize that information immediately. So, let's say, for example, a design issue held up work from being completed that week. I'll make a phone call to my architect directly after the meeting letting him know that a design decision is delaying work. If it's a material or manpower issue, then I'm making a call to the trade partner's office and following up with an email letting them know that a commitment was not kept due to material or manpower. I use the data I have in real-time, and I document and ask for recovery plans way sooner than I ever did before.

"What I have noticed from our trade partners is the squeaky wheel with the most data gets the oil. What I mean is, when a general contractor gets behind schedule, they always ask for more manpower. Our trade partners know that some superintendents have no flow in their projects and it's not a *manpower issue*, but a *workflow issue*. But with the Last Planner System, the visual communication tools, and the boards showing exactly *what the commitments are* and *when they are due*, there is nowhere to hide."

Sam was excited about what he was hearing. As Alan pulled up to his house at dusk, he thanked him for everything—the fishing, the conversation, and the storytelling. He couldn't wait to implement PPC with his team in the coming week.

Sam arrived at the jobsite Monday morning focused on execution. There were roughly seven weeks left in the project, and he was committed to delivering. After the daily huddle Monday morning, Sam held the last planners back and explained the concept of PPC. The trade partners seemed a bit reluctant, but with all the other changes Sam had implemented thus far, they were ready to roll with the punches—especially if they thought it would help them get to the finish line. They felt a sense of pride and commitment, unlike on other projects they had worked on, and they really wanted to see this job through.

Overall, the week was productive as they cruised into the Friday huddle meeting. After each trade went through their routine daily huddle discussion points, Sam moved up to the board and grabbed a dry erase marker. "All right, guys, let's give this a shot! Hank, you're up. Item one: Complete or Not Complete? Did you get all the flex tied into the ceiling diffusers on the second floor?"

Hank affirmed it was done.

"Great!" Sam encouraged. "Item two: did you get all the grills installed in the restrooms on the second floor?"

Hank happily reported that these were done as well.

Sam thanked Hank and then moved through all of Bobby's items; these were also complete. From there, Sam turned to Tom. "OK, item one: did you turn down all the fire sprinkler lines on the second floor in Areas A & B?"

"Yes, sir," Tom said, smiling. "All but the ones above the nurses' stations. We'll turn those down on Monday. Put me down for one hundred percent!"

"Sorry, Tom, I'm not picking on you, but that is a zero percent," Sam said reluctantly, as he wrote *No* next to Tom's commitment on the board.

Tom frowned. "What do you mean, Sam? It's just two little areas, and we can knock those out by Monday."

"I know, Tom, and I do understand what you're saying," Sam offered reassuringly. "But if you remember what I explained on Monday, the PPC is not *tracking production* but *measuring commitments*. Since you weren't able to turn all the heads down this week as promised on Monday, Bobby will not be able to start Areas A & B nurses' stations next Monday as he had planned. You not meeting your commitment may not impact *you* that much, but you have to remember what it could affect *downstream*."

Tom understood what Sam was saying. "OK, Sam, I hear you. I'm still getting use to this PPC thing, but that makes sense to me."

Sam continued down the roster until he made it through the rest of the team. He pulled up his calculator app and punched in his numbers.

"We got seventy-five percent! Not bad, boys. Now, let's look at the root cause for why the twenty-five percent was not completed. Tom, let's start with you. Out of this list of root causes, what was the main reason you didn't get the heads turned down in the nurses' stations this week?"

Tom reviewed the list:

- Weather
- Manpower
- Machinery
- Design
- Make-ready needs
- Materials
- Poor scheduling

"Well, I hate to say it, but it was poor scheduling on my part. I just thought we'd be able to hit it. I'll be a little less ambitious in my commitments next week."

"Fair enough," said Sam.

The team identified all of the root causes for failed commitments that week. Out of the twenty commitments promised by the team, the last planners delivered on fifteen of them. The root causes for missed commitments were comprised of:

1 – Poor scheduling
2 – Manpower
1 – Material
1 – Make-ready needs

Sam scribbled the score and root causes in his notepad and then explained that he was going to ask Gene to send emails to each of their offices letting them know that the team needed support with manpower, materials, and buy-in on the team's recovery plans for the missed commitments that week. As the trades disbanded and went back into the field, Bobby lingered behind.

"Sam, at the start of this job and through all of the ups and downs, I wasn't quite sure what to think of you or these crazy ideas you were throwing our way. But I want you to know that you have helped me change how I look at my work, and I'm really bought in to this Lean stuff."

Sam put his hand on Bobby's shoulder. "I appreciate that, Bobby. I've changed the way I look at our work, too. Let's just hope it's not too late for us to get this thing finished on time!"

Over the next few weeks, the team really began to hit their stride. The field was more accountable to each other than they ever had been before; each of the last planners understood what their commitments meant to the team and the overall impact to the project as they approached their substantial completion date.

Sam pulled into the grocery store parking lot at 5:30 p.m. on Friday to fulfill a request for a jar of pickles and some strawberry ice cream. After dinner, he gave Jen a foot massage and, when she had fallen asleep, he went in his office to wrap up some daily reports that he'd fallen behind on. His mind quickly turned to the success he was having on the project over the last few weeks and the Percent Plan Complete process. He wondered if there was a way to make the PPC scores more visual.

He pulled out his notepad and started to sketch a pie chart and a dot matrix for a twelve-week period. He wondered if he would have success enlarging it and making it into another visual board, similar to the boards Alan had in his Big Room. Sam thought that, if the team saw the score week-to-week and the root causes for work not being complete, maybe it could help motivate them and create even more accountability.

Determined to make his idea come to life, Sam stopped off at the reprographics store on Monday morning. When Friday rolled around, Bobby was the first to comment on his new board. "Sam, if you keep adding boards you are going to run out of wall space!"

Sam laughed. "This is my control panel, Bobby! With this dashboard, we know everything we need to know about how this project is running: who is working where, what the constraints are, if the commitments are being made or not...it's all *right here*."

Bobby admired the boards with Sam. When the trades finished talking about their work for that day, Sam went through the PPC Q&A session again—but this time, Sam colored in the percentage of commitments made in the circle pie chart he had created, and tracked the root cause for work not being completed on the visual board.

"This will help keep us accountable," Sam explained. All of the last planners agreed and were on board with utilizing the PPC board Sam had created. With less than a month left in the project, Sam had no choice but to put all his trust into the Last Planner System—and in the last planners themselves.

Whatever the outcome, he knew that from now on this was the only way he was going to work. He was committed to always look for ways to "sharpen his axe."

Epilogue

Sam pulled up to his project at 6:30 a.m. on Monday and turned off his engine. The parking lot was now paved, and the landscapers were making their way around the building, installing irrigation and plants. He paused for a minute before getting out of his truck. *Only a couple of Mondays left, and the project will be done,* he thought. He couldn't believe how fast the time was flying by. As he entered the trailer, he realized that he needed to make plans to demobilize the trailer and CONEXs.

He put his bag in his office, started the coffee pot, and went over to review his boards. This had become customary for him, and he was already having a hard time remembering how he started his day before. As he reviewed the three-week look-ahead board—the last-ever three-week look-ahead board for this project—he was pleased with what he and his team had been working so hard to achieve: a path to completion. It was right there, and everyone could taste it.

At 6:55 a.m. on the dot the trades started to fill up the trailer, and at 7:00 a.m. the guys dug into their huddle. As Sam watched the trades go over their items and interact with each other, he thought it looked like they had been doing this for years. The team was solid, their workflow was smooth, and the constraints were becoming fewer and fewer.

All except for one.

"Sam, we've been waiting on these doors for the first floor to show up for a few weeks now. Where are they?" Bobby asked.

Gene, who began attending the huddles over the last few months, spoke up. "I'm sorry about this, Bobby. The doors were released months ago, and I haven't been getting straight answers as to why the remaining doors and hardware for the first floor are late. What I do know is that they are being loaded up today and are expected to be onsite before the week is done."

"'*Before the week is done*'?" Bobby repeated, frustrated. "We are running out of time, and I'm worried about getting the doors swinging, hardwared out, and tied-in to the low voltage systems before finals. If we don't get the doors and hardware this week, it's going to be tough to make it, guys."

Gene looked at Sam and then back at Bobby. "I get it. I'm worried, too, and wish I had better news than that."

●●●

Sam was finishing daily reports late Thursday evening when he heard the air brakes release on a semi delivery truck. He peeked out the window and was excited to see that the doors and hardware had finally arrived. Grabbing his hard hat, he quickly made his way over to meet the delivery driver to begin inventorying the delivery.

"Boy, am I glad to see you!" he told the driver, relieved. But as Sam's eyes scanned over the packing slip, his heart began to sink.

"Hey, buddy, looking at this slip, I'm only seeing doors on this delivery. Where is the hardware?!"

The truck driver looked at the slip and shrugged. "Sorry, man, I'm just the driver. All I have is what's on the truck. You'll need to take it up with the manufacturer who shipped the delivery."

Sam helped the driver unload the doors and then called Gene.

"What's up?"

"'What's up' is we have a big problem." Sam said miserably. "We just got the delivery of the doors, but *without the hardware.*"

"All right, Sam. It's late, but I'll fire an email off tonight and call first thing to see what's up. Hopefully they are just on another tracking number and still coming out before Friday."

"*Tomorrow is Friday,* Gene!" Sam insisted. "If we don't get them, we're going to have a major problem on our hands."

"Sorry, Sam, I'm on it," Gene reassured, even though he couldn't help but feel doomed, too.

Sam had trouble sleeping that night and was wide awake at 4:00 a.m. His mind was restless, thinking that, after all they had been through and all they had learned, this could be the one thing that wouldn't allow the team to finish the project. He couldn't stop dwelling on how he was going to deliver the message to Bobby and the team. Sam gave up on sleep and rolled out of bed to get dressed and head into work.

●●●

Bobby grinned at Sam when he came into the trailer to get fresh coffee before the huddle started. "Hey, I saw the doors onsite this morning!" he said cheerily. "This is great! I was worried; talk about cutting it too close for comfort..."

Sam interrupted him. "Bobby, we still have a big problem. I'm hoping to have more info from Gene this morning, but we only got *the doors* yesterday. *No hardware.*"

"You have to be kidding me!" moaned Bobby. "That's it! We're not going to make it..."

"No, we'll make it. I'm sure Gene will have something within the hour," Sam said, trying to sound confident. But the look on Bobby's face made Sam think his voice was wavering.

The huddle went great and the team scored a ninety percent PPC score with the only missed commitment being the installation of the doors and hardware on the first floor of Area C. Unfortunately, Sam couldn't celebrate any of the team's successes, because without those doors swinging there was no way the city's building inspector was going to give him a Certificate of Occupancy.

After the huddle, Sam checked his phone. Nothing. He called Gene; no answer.

Sam tried to stay calm and went out into the field to make sure everything else was still on track. As Sam entered the front door of the medical office building, his pocket started to vibrate. It was Gene.

"Give me good news!" he answered.

"Sorry I missed your call, Sam. I was talking to Pete Finch at Osbourne Doors. The hardware was just loaded up on a truck somewhere in Pennsylvania. They are doing a quick ship, but that still doesn't get it here until Monday or Tuesday."

Sam was irate. "This is a bunch of garbage. They're sinking me! The fire marshal told me last week that we will not pass inspection with temporary hardware."

"I know. I'm sorry, Sam. I told them this was unacceptable, but it's out of our control at this point."

"Gene, if the hardware comes in Monday evening, we would have to have it all installed by mid-day Thursday to get remaining finals Thursday afternoon for Certificate of Occupancy by Friday. Bobby had originally planned four or five days for this work; I can't see how they can possibly get it done in that window. We have lead-lined pivot-hinged doors in the MRI room, and the corridor doors remaining on the first floor are Stanley-operated double egress fire-rated doors that are tied into the badge readers and security interface...those take tons of time. Even if they *could* get it done, *one missed inspection and the schedule's blown.* And what if it's not all on the truck, or if it's really not coming at all?" Sam despaired.

"Sam, I'll make a call to Bobby's office to see if they can help get more installers. I will also call around to some of our other interior trade partners to see if they have resources to help supplement crews."

"OK. Thanks, Gene," Sam said helplessly. "I'll let the team know."

The hardware arrived early afternoon on Monday and all pieces were accounted for. Working together, Bobby and Gene managed to get a few additional resources from Bobby's office and a small crew from another interior trade partner. It was going to be tight. The doors had to be completed by Friday morning to ensure the fire final would pass. The plan was to work late that evening shaking everything out and staging the appropriate door and corresponding hardware to each door opening, then getting all door hardware installed and low voltage hooked up by Thursday morning to be ready for the fire marshal's inspection, paving the path to the Certificate of Occupancy on Friday. The only good thing Sam had going for him was that all other finals had passed, and the cleaning crews were hard at work making the place shine.

At the Tuesday huddle, the conversation was entirely focused on the doors.

"Sam, our guys worked until midnight last night, but things aren't looking good," Bobby reported grimly. "We were all supposed to be back today, ready to go at 6:00 a.m., but one of my crews has not shown up. It may have been too much of an ask, considering how late they worked. With forty-eight hours remaining it just doesn't look like we can get there. I'm sorry."

The room was quiet. Sam had nothing to say. He felt like he had exhausted all of his options and it was time to face the music.

"Bobby, what do you need to get to the finish line?" Roberto asked.

Bobby quickly thought through some calculations. "I think I can get there if we had four more guys who could install hardware."

"OK," Roberto responded. "Where do you need me?"

"What do you mean?" Bobby asked.

"I used to be a carpenter, and I know how to hang doors," Roberto answered authoritatively. Then he turned to face the rest of the group and added, "We have made it this far as a team, now we need to get this thing across the finish line!"

"Really, Roberto?" asked Sam, who was stunned. "You'd do that?"

"Yeah, I want to help," Roberto affirmed.

"I want to help, too," Tom chimed in. "I have a guy who used to be a carpenter as well. I could have him report to Bobby to assist with anything he needed."

"I can't hang doors," offered Hank, "but I'll help out any way I can!"

"Same here," agreed Jim.

Bobby was jubilant. "Thanks, you guys! I really appreciate this."

Speechless, Sam watched his team rally together for the betterment of the project. As the huddle wrapped up, Bobby got a call from his office notifying him that two more guys were being pulled from another project and headed his way. Just like that, the team had hope they might make it after all.

●●●

After a grueling forty-eight hours with little sleep, the team had managed to get the doors swinging and systems tied in by Thursday. The fire final went off without a hitch on Thursday afternoon, and Sam was on pins and needles all day Friday waiting for the building inspector to arrive. After what seemed like an eternity, she finally showed up at 2:00 p.m. on Friday and they began their walk. Exactly one hour later, the inspection was done. They passed! Sam was overwhelmed with emotion. The team had done it, and he couldn't be prouder. He thanked the building official and called Gene.

"Gene! We did it! We passed!" Sam crowed.

"Awesome, Sam! I will call St. Claire right now and let them know."

"This is huge! Let's gather the guys to go celebrate!"

Sam hung up and he started to call Alan with the good news when his phone vibrated. His wife's picture popped up on his screen.

"SAM!" Jen shouted. "MY WATER BROKE!!"

Twelve hours later, and Sam was a new father. His mind was reeling—Jen's due date was still two weeks away, yet here they were, surrounded by family and passing a little stranger around the hospital room. He had never seen Jen so happy, and he'd certainly never felt so happy himself.

They were back home the next day, and things were finally quiet after the last of Jen's sisters had left. Sam had his choice of no less than five different casseroles to heat up for dinner; he picked one that looked good and stuck it in the oven. He checked on Jen and the baby, who were sound asleep, and then pulled out his phone to text Alan:

Juggernaut is here! Can you come over tomorrow afternoon?

Alan wrote back that he would leave his site early, put on a clean shirt, and come right over.

Sam heard the gravel crunching under tires in the driveway, and he went to open the door. Alan was carrying something...and Sam laughed when he realized it was another casserole.

"Elsie's tuna noodle specialty!" Alan said, handing it over. "She's going to come by in the morning, but she wanted you to have this now."

"Excellent, I'll heat it up for all of us here in a little while," Sam replied gratefully. "But first, I want you to meet someone."

Alan followed Sam into the nursery. The walls were painted light blue with wispy, white clouds and bunches of colorful balloons flying by. A bookshelf was filled with new books and rows of stuffed toys, and the crib was pristine white against the wall under the window where the late afternoon sun glowed bright. Sam gestured to a stuffed rocking chair and told Alan to have a seat, and then he lifted the baby from the crib.

"This is my son," Sam said, kneeling and placing the infant into Alan's arms. "This is Andrew."

The men were quiet as Alan slowly rocked the baby. After a few minutes, Alan reached into his back pocket to pull out a neatly folded handkerchief so he could blow his nose. He placed his hand on Sam's shoulder and looked in his eyes and, in that moment, so many things passed between them that no words needed to be said.

A week passed by in what felt like a couple of days. It was Sunday afternoon; Jen was enjoying a long shower and Andrew was swaddled on Sam's chest as he rocked him back and forth in his nursery. Sam was returning to work the next day, and his mind began to wander to the St. Claire's project team; how unbelievable that journey was, and how proud he was to be a part of—and help to lead—a team that had so much respect for one another that they would go above and beyond their own scope and responsibilities to help the overall job succeed.

As he thought through all Alan had taught him, it became clear how intentional Alan was in teaching him the right lessons and the right Lean tools at just the right moments. In retrospect, it was evident to Sam that you had to start with baby steps when embarking on your Lean journey, and that's exactly what Alan did for him. First, he got Sam's attention by challenging him to try a daily huddle in lieu of a long, weekly trade partner meeting to better facilitate coordination and accountability amongst the trades. Then Sam started to buy-in even more after Alan explained the importance of tangible communication tools to make the construction trailer a visual workspace that allowed the team to bridge communication gaps and facilitate better trade-to-trade collaboration. Learning about, and being able to identify, the "Eight Deadly Wastes" on the jobsite also completely transformed the way in which he viewed work in the field, and allowed the team to pinpoint root causes for field issues much faster, thus allowing the team to resolve constraints and challenges more effectively without getting sidetracked by the noise around the issues.

However, it wasn't until he started managing constraints visually with the team that they began to solve issues on a higher level by adding a layer of accountability that he had not personally experienced before. Sam was amazed how much he'd already transformed before implementing Alan's final lesson, which was the Last Planner System. Thinking back, if Alan would have showed him Pull Planning, Look-Ahead Plans, Weekly Work Plans, and Percent Plan Complete at the very beginning, it would have been very likely that the team would not have been ready for that level of collaboration and accountability.

The real icing on the cake, though, was how much Alan taught him about respect for people, like valuing the contributions that the design teams and trade partners brought to the table, and always looking for proactive ways to be the best team player you could be for the betterment of the overall project.

Sam put Andrew down in his crib and quietly closed the door, and then he walked over to his office to fire up his laptop. He wanted to look at his calendar for the coming week and clean up a few emails. As he scrolled through his inbox, he noticed an interesting subject line on an unread email from Gene:

To Sam – The Lean Builder

Opening the email, Sam found there was no text, just a single image attachment—Gene had taken a picture of all of the last planners gathered in front of Sam's boards and visual tools. They were smiling happily and holding a giant stuffed "Elmo" teddy bear with a red bow tie and a tag tied to his neck that read: *For Andrew.*

Sam smiled to himself. As he closed his laptop, he thought, *The Lean Builder...I like the sound of that.*

The Playbook

We hope you enjoyed *The Lean Builder*. As field-focused Lean practitioners, we were motivated to explain the concepts, tools, and principles of Lean in an engaging fable format to help you—project superintendents and last planners—see the implementation of Lean tools and concepts in an easy-to-read, familiar way based on day-to-day life on a jobsite.

While the concepts laid out in the book may seem easy to follow, we wanted to take it a step further by sharing with you what we call "The Playbook." This is a step-by-step, how-to guide based on years of trial and error and Builder's Lean experience. Our hope is that you can take this playbook and easily begin to implement these best practices on your jobsites to not only improve production and workflow, but to give you hours back in your day by working *smarter*, not *harder*.

Before you get started, an important note. If you are new to Lean and this is your first time trying out these new tools and processes, please take this advice:

Start small.
In beginning this journey, we strongly encourage you to start small with baby steps. The chapters in this book were strategically

laid out, starting with a morning huddle and building up to the Last Planner System. This was intentional. Please resist the urge to jump ahead. Take your time and master each "play" before moving on to the next.

Keep your head up!

Lean concepts are simple, but implementation is not easy. You will fail a time or two, trade foremen will push back—and when things on your project get tough, it will be very easy to go for the escape hatch and return to what is familiar. We encourage you to keep your head up and stay the course. Implementing Lean tools and processes on a jobsite takes perseverance and determination. Trust us when we tell you the payoff is worth it. You will reap the benefit tenfold of whatever effort you invest in this journey.

#1. The Daily Huddle

Do your "subcontractor" or "field coordination" meetings seem unproductive? Do your trade partner foremen seem disengaged? Do topics take too long to close out—and when the meeting adjourns, do you feel like not much was accomplished?

If you answered "yes" to any of these questions, it might be time to shake things up with a daily huddle.

Whether you start or finish your day with a huddle, this meeting structure will facilitate more efficient communication, collaboration, and accountability. This section of The Playbook will offer you guidelines to implement an effective daily huddle.

Keep it short.
A daily huddle should last no longer than fifteen-twenty minutes. Any longer than that, and you risk losing the attention and engagement of the meeting participants. An egg timer is a useful tool to help get the team into the practice and rhythm of a short meeting. This may seem strange to get used to at first, but the team will quickly realize what is most important and worth talking about during the brief daily huddle time.

Start on time, and end on time.
There is a lot of value in starting and finishing your meeting on time. It fosters productivity, it makes a good first impression, and it shows you value your attendees' time. And by continuously enforcing the promised time restraints, you demonstrate follow-through in keeping your word.

No phones or distractions.

Everyone should participate and be engaged. Allowing participants to use their phones at the huddles shows a lack of respect to the team because it sets the expectation that the information on your phone is more important than the conversation in the meeting.

Stand up.

Remove the chairs from the meeting space so that everyone is standing. This will help keep everyone engaged as well as helping everyone stay focused on the topic/discussion at hand. If they are sitting back in a comfortable chair, attendees are more inclined to disengage and turn off their brains.

Get in a routine.

Have the trade leaders get in the habit of routinely answering the following questions at the daily huddle:

1. What are you working on?
2. Where are you working?
3. How many crews/workers are on-site?
4. What are your constraints/needs?
5. What material deliveries are coming up?

By asking these five questions, you are engaging the trade partners and allowing them to collaborate and coordinate with the other trades. This achieves buy-in and accountability and allows for a more reliable workflow.

Stay on track.

Without intent and discipline, it is very easy for a daily huddle to get off track. It is important to know which problems or conversations *are not* critical to moving the huddle forward. To maximize value, use the following terminology to make sure the time is well spent:

- **Two Minute Rule / ELMO** – If a topic has run its course, if a point has been made and it is time to move on, or if the issue or circumstance does not involve the entire team and can be resolved at a later time, any member of the huddle is empowered to call the Two Minute Rule, or ELMO (the two terms are interchangeable).

  The Two Minute Rule means that the issue has been discussed for two minutes or longer and it needs to be put aside for now and resolved outside of the huddle. ELMO stands for *Enough, Let's Move On*—playfully tossing a stuffed animal you've named "Elmo" at the speaker can be a fun way to break the tension of cutting someone off.

- **The Parking Lot** – Once the Two Minute Rule or ELMO has been called, those items need to be placed in "the parking lot." (It is good practice to write parking lot items on a whiteboard as they arise so that they are not forgotten about.) Placing items in the parking lot means that a quick discussion will be held following the huddle with the affected people in order to discuss the issues or circumstances that did not require everyone's involvement.

Involve the entire team.
Meetings will be even more productive if the general contractor's project manager, assistant project manager, and/or project

engineer are available to attend. They may have relevant information that the rest of the team does not have, and their participation can help provide faster resolutions on constraints that may involve the input of the design team or owner. When the trades see that the entire team is active in the process, it fosters buy-in.

#2. Visual Communication

Visual communication plays a very important role in establishing and maintaining a reliable workflow in the field. When communication breaks down on a jobsite, teams will experience loss of productivity, hindered completion times, and costly errors. Visual communication tools will significantly help to bridge communication gaps and facilitate better trade-to-trade collaboration at the morning huddle. It will also help build accountability amongst all team members.

Once you have gained traction with your daily huddles, implement the following to make your trailer a visual workspace:

Floor Plans/Elevations Under Laminate + Dry Erase Markers
Purchase clear laminate and a pack of dry erase markers with multiple colors. Designate a different color per trade. Place floor plans and elevations under laminate, and have trade partners verbally and visually show the entire team the following at the daily huddle:

1. What they are working on;
2. Where they are working;
3. How many crews/workers are on-site;
4. Where there are constraints;
5. What material deliveries are coming up.

By using dry erase markers that are color-coded to their work, marking up the floor plans on the wall as a team is one of the simplest ways to visually communicate all planned activities with all construction trades on the jobsite.

Material Delivery & Inspection Boards

Material Delivery and Inspection Boards were not discussed in our story, but these tools take visual communication a step further.

Material Delivery Board

Material Delivery visual boards are a great way to ensure that project deliveries are "just in time," which is a system for producing or delivering the right amount of parts or product at the time it is needed for production.

Create a weekly dry erase calendar board that has each day of the week shown and enough space to accommodate multiple deliveries. The material delivery board should be used to help the trades answer the following questions:

1. What is being delivered?
2. What time is it being delivered?
3. What company is delivering it?
4. What type of truck is it coming in?
5. Where will it be unloaded?
6. How will it be unloaded (by hand, by lift, by crane, etc.)?

By communicating this information visually, it allows all team members to know the logistics of building materials coming onto the site and can potentially avoid many of the Eight Wastes (these are explained in the final section of The Playbook).

Inspection Board

Inspection boards can help everyone onsite know when project inspection dates are occurring and what the current status is, which can help with productivity onsite. Create a weekly dry erase calendar board that has each day of the week shown and enough space to accommodate multiple inspections. The inspection board should answer the following questions:

1. What is the inspection/what is being inspected?
2. Who requested the inspection?
3. What date/time was the inspection requested?
4. What date/time will the inspection occur?
5. What are the results of the inspection?

Virtual Design in Construction (VDC) & Building Information Modeling (BIM)

VDC and BIM were not discussed in our story, but these tools take visual communication a step further. Depending on the complexity of your project, using a TV monitor and a 3D model helps everyone visualize the 2D design. The use of these visual communication tools can also help sidestep a foreign language barrier that might exist with some construction foremen.

You may recognize other needs for visual communication in the trailer or on your jobsite and decide to try out other boards that you create yourself. If so, you need to make sure that your visual tools are always easy to:

— Set up
— See
— Update/maintain
— Use
— Understand

#3. Managing Constraints

Have there been times on a jobsite where you felt overwhelmed by a barrage of issues? Do you ever find it difficult to understand, organize, and remove these problems in an effective manner? If so, a constraint board can help.

A constraint board is a powerful tool that can help the team to communicate, prioritize, and track the constraints that arise during construction. Here are the steps to follow if you'd like to successfully implement a constraint board at your daily huddles:

Creating a Constraint Board
Obtain a laminated piece of paper or a whiteboard that can be written on with dry erase markers, two feet by three feet in size, with the following columns:

- What
- Where
- Who
- When

You also need some dry erase markers in a variety of colors, each color representing a specific trade partner. Keeping a spray cleaning solution and a rag for wiping down the board handy is useful, since the store-bought erasers get worn out quickly (which is a good thing, as this means the team is collaborating and removing each other's constraints, yielding a more reliable workflow).

Implementing a Constraint Board
Constraints will be identified during the normal course of conversation during your daily huddles. How diligent and

thoughtful you are about capturing and organizing these constraints will determine how successful you are in making the board effective. The following guidelines will help.

What/Where?

When a last planner brings up a new constraint in the daily huddle, it is important to not get too deep in the details of the constraint at first. The huddles are fast-paced, and a lot of time can be spent while describing a constraint and its implications. It is best to just fill out the *what* column to start and have the team move on. When the huddle is over and the constraint is explored further, more details around *what* and *where* can be added for clarity.

Who/When?

The *who* and *when* columns must be filled out at the huddle with the last planners. This is the commitment portion of the constraint board; assigning the responsibility for resolving a constraint to someone and having that person make a commitment about when it will be resolved adds strong layers of accountability to the team. This is needed to effectively help the workflow downstream, allowing for the team members to plan and commit with confidence.

Share the Responsibility

At the daily huddle, challenge your teams to write their own constraints on the board. This will allow the trade with the constraint to feel like they have a voice—*because they do*—and feel that they are being heard, valued, and respected by the others on their team. This behavior will soon begin to shift the project's culture into one where the trades *collaborate and resolve their issues together*, rather than making the superintendent the middleman. This removes a significant amount of waste from the previous constraint resolution process.

Review Daily

Even though many constraints will take longer than one day to resolve, make it a habit to review the constraint board with the project team every day at the huddle. This helps remind everyone of the current constraints, allows for new constraints to be added, and allows for those responsible for a constraint to report their progress or announce that a constraint has been removed.

Removing Constraints

Only the person who initiated the constraint should be allowed to remove the constraint. This allows the initiator to maintain ownership over the constraint they identified and prevents a constraint from being removed by someone who may not have all of the necessary information.

Develop and Leverage Your Soft Skills

This constraint process will be tough for some team members to get used to, as many are not used to this level of transparency or accountability. If you are facilitating the meeting and listening to a constraint being raised to the team, be aware of how you are engaging the trade partner. Remember to listen carefully and understand the issue at hand. It is important to use self-awareness to understand others when challenges and conflicts are being raised, as those individuals are often in an overextended state.

Build the Project Culture

Despite the team's best efforts, you may have an outlier or two who will not get on board with this new tool. Be aware you may have to motivate or incentivize a behavior change, or possibly make a leadership change if the overall jobsite or team culture is being negatively impacted.

At the heart of the Lean philosophy is respect for the individual. If you take a step back, the construction industry is primarily comprised of relationships, commitments, and problem-solving. What sets the great teams apart is respecting people and accepting them where they are, and focusing on solving the root causes instead of on the noise that surrounds the challenges or constraints.

#4. The Last Planner System®

Once you feel that your team is having a strong daily huddle where visual communication tools and a constraint board have been implemented, it is time to move on to the Last Planner System. This can be overwhelming at first; however, once you begin this journey and start leveraging the power and efficiency of this operating system, you will create significant value for yourself and your team.

The beauty of this operating system is that *it allows the field leaders closest to the work to plan the work*. These leaders are the *last planners*.

The Last Planner System is holistic, and all facets of it must be utilized to leverage its maximum potential. It is broken out into five components:

1. **Master Scheduling**
2. **Phase Scheduling**
3. **Look Ahead Planning**
4. **Weekly Work Planning**
5. **Percent Plan Complete**

Master Scheduling is what most of us in the industry have done for years: building a project schedule from start to finish and identifying the project milestones. These schedules are typically built by the general contractor, often with little or no input from the trade partners.

In our business, most contracts are signed between an owner and a general contractor based on the Master Schedule. The main issue in our industry is that this is usually where the scheduling process stops. The general contractor will either issue this same schedule, no schedule, or a shortened schedule to the trades without asking for their input.

The Last Planner System changes this status quo with the next component, Phase Scheduling.

Phase Scheduling is collaborative planning which produces better schedules because the schedule is being built, collectively, by the experts who will perform the work. With the benefit of the trade partners' input and buy-in, phase scheduling is a game-changer when it comes to building a reliable schedule. Pull planning is a Lean tool that last planners will leverage during the phase scheduling component of the Last Planner System. Pull planning and phase scheduling are often referred to as one and the same; however, the pull plan is the vehicle or process that drives the collaboration and reliable commitments at this stage.

It takes time to execute a well-run pull plan that not only accomplishes a dependable schedule, but that also leaves everyone understanding the schedule and the commitments they have made. The steps to ensure a high-quality pull plan session follow.

What you need:

- A big room with adequate wall space.

- Several different colors of sticky note pads (a different color for each trade) and enough markers for the trades to write down their activities, durations, and handoffs.

- Somewhere to place the sticky notes (whiteboard, an empty wall, or a roll of plotter paper secured with painter's tape, clips, magnets, etc.)

- A second whiteboard or sheet of plotter paper to capture constraints *(issues that need to be resolved to release work)*; and a parking lot *(the items that need to be discussed but do not directly impact the schedule or need everyone's involvement in the room).*

- Construction documents, like drawings and specs, site plans, floor plans, the BIM model, and other visual communication documents for the trades to refer to when planning.

- A printed copy of the project's master schedule for transparency and to reference.

- A posted copy of the contractual master schedule to refer to in regard to overall project duration and milestones.

Before the Pull Plan session:

- **Decide on the milestone to pull**—Do not be overly ambitious. A twelve-to-sixteen-week pull plan meeting for teams unfamiliar with the process can be overwhelming. Long pull plans have the tendency to frustrate trade partners and can lead to teams not feeling like much value was added.

- **Decide on a facilitator**—If possible, choose a facilitator that is neutral to the project. This can help allow for better collaboration. If the project superintendent facilitates the pull plan, be sure that they do not try to dictate activities, as this can lead to trade partners feeling pressured to make commitments to activities that are unattainable. The facilitator's role is crucial to the success of the pull plan, and a good facilitator will be able to lead the team, ask good questions, and keep everyone on track.

- **Select who should attend**—When you have selected the date for your pull plan, be mindful of who is invited. Last planners (the people that make assignments to direct the work, i.e. foremen/superintendents) are *required*. If trade partner project managers are making commitments at the pull plan in lieu of the last planner installing the work, there is a chance that durations will be incorrect. However, trade partner project managers are encouraged to attend, especially if they have a better understanding of the status of material fabrication and delivery. From the general contractor's side, be sure that superintendents and project management staff are invited and in attendance.

- **Pre-Pull**—It is advised for the general contractor to do a pre-pull plan meeting before doing one with all the trade partners in attendance. This allows the superintendent and project management teams to discuss expectations, predicted work durations, and share their thoughts around the direction of workflow and phasing.

  Note: the direction of the pull plan can deviate from the pre-pull, and that's okay. It is just important to have thought through the phasing and scheduling as a team prior to the meeting; that is the purpose of the pre-pull.

By pre-pulling the project, the general contractor can develop a "cheat sheet" that allows them to monitor key durations during the pull plan and challenge the team when needed to ensure float is not being built into any activities.

The last step in doing an internal pre-pull plan is developing a template that can be emailed to trade partners, along with the construction documents/BIM models, that clearly articulates:

- Date, time, and purpose of the pull plan;
- Expectations around who should attend and what each person will contribute;
- Preliminary thoughts around work phasing and flow;
- Desired level of detail that should be described for each activity.

- **Determine the length of the meeting**—It is recommended not to schedule a pull plan that lasts more than two-to-three hours. Last planners will begin to lose concentration and become disengaged. If needed, a complex pull can be broken out into multiple sessions over several days. When sending out the invitation to the meeting, be specific about the time required to achieve a successful planning session.

- **Set up the meeting room**—*(Refer to "what you need" above for requisite materials.)*
  Be sure that the room is set up and ready in advance. Best practices and recommendations include:

a. Set up the pull boards. You may be using a whiteboard, mounted plotter paper, or a pre-printed calendar board with swim lanes; just be sure that they are set up with adequate space to plan. Make sure the top column is showing the number of either the day or the week, but try to avoid having calendar days. Be sure to provide enough columns so that you do not run short.

b. Establish a whiteboard or mounted paper designated for constraints or parking lot items.

c. Have an ample quantity of sticky pads and markers for the trades to use. Try to have a different color sticky pad for each trade. Make sure the markers are in good working order.

d. Chairs are optional. Some teams engage better when everyone is up and standing at the boards, and some teams do better when they can sit and strategize, then stand up and post cards. Try both options and see which works best for your teams.

e. Lower the temperature in the room. Once you have a lot of people gathered, it will get much warmer. You need everyone to be comfortable so they can focus on the work that needs to be done.

Running a Pull Plan Session:
As you approach the day of the pull plan, be sure you remind the trade partners of the day, time, and duration of the meeting by

phone or email. If even one critical trade partner is missing, it will derail the pull plan, so it is imperative that attendance for critical trades is perfect. Below are best practices for running an effective pull plan session.

Part One – Pull plan introductions & ground rules

- Once the trades arrive and have signed in, the facilitator should ask the attendees to introduce themselves.

- The facilitator should poll the room to understand who has been involved in a pull plan session before and who has not. This will help them identify who may need more coaching and guidance during the session.

- The facilitator needs to describe to the team what pull planning is and make sure everyone understands that *the team will work from the end milestone back to the starting milestone.*

- The facilitator will emphasize goals for the session in order to:

  - plan collaboratively;
  - make commitments to one another on the tasks, durations, and handoffs;
  - optimize flow;
  - identify, discuss, and solve constraints that may affect commitments.

Part Two – Filling out cards

a. Be sure that each trade partner has a different color sticky pad and that they write the name of their trade on top. Another option is to have stickies premade that segment the trade name, activity, duration, and handoff.

b. As trades begin filling out their cards, the facilitator should help the team think through their workflow in a push sequence, since it is sometimes difficult for last planners to think in a pull sequence when just getting started.

c. The facilitator should make sure everyone understands that for every card there is a predecessor card, and that the "handoff" is what is needed to be complete before work can start.

d. The facilitator should remind the team that the cards should have enough detail on them so that if someone who did not attend the session read the card, they should easily understand the activity, duration, and handoff.

e. Make sure that no durations take longer than ten days. If they do, have the last planners break it into multiple cards to allow succeeding activities to begin sooner, which can optimize the schedule.

f. The facilitator's job, while trades are filling out cards, is to work their way around the room making sure that the last planner's questions are being answered and the information being required is adequate and legible.

Part Three – Posting cards and pulling back

- Have trade partners come up to the board and start by placing the final activity at the end (far right side of the pull plan board). Make sure the teams know the cards are based on the end of the activity and represent the final day of the activity, not the beginning.

- As trades place their cards on the board, pulling back from the final activity, it is good practice to use "swim lanes," which may be allocated by sequence, area, or trade. The goal with swim lanes is to help organize the information to make sure people do not get confused or lost in the planning process.

- The facilitator should help trades post cards when needed, and make sure the last planners are interacting and verbally stating what handoff they need completed to begin their work. They should also be doing quality control to make sure the cards are being placed on the board correctly. Finally, the facilitator should monitor the room to make sure everyone is engaged and that there is not a lot of unrelated conversation.

Part Four – The recap

a. Once all the pull plan cards are on the wall and the critical handoffs are established and committed to, the facilitator will walk the team backwards through the logic one last time asking for a verbal confirmation that the trade partners agree with the durations and the necessary handoffs for the work to completed.

b. The facilitator must confirm/check to see if the duration meets the contractual duration. It is important that last planners do not add any buffer or float to their durations, as it could have major impacts to the schedule.

If the pull plan shows a shorter duration of time than the original schedule, those extra days will be considered "team float," that can either be used to offset missed commitments throughout the milestone or be used in future milestone phases.

If the duration is longer, the team will review durations card by card to fully ensure there is no built-in float and look for ways to re-phase or allow critical path items to begin sooner. This can be done by breaking longer duration cards into more activities. Sometimes this can be done in the same meeting, and sometimes this needs to be done in another session based on how long and tedious the pull plan was. If the team decides there is no other way to re-phase work or work extra hours to complete the original duration, then the team will know that they will have to look to make up those extra days in a future pull plan session.

a. After recapping the pull, the facilitator will read through the constraint list where items that need to be resolved to allow the flow sequencing to occur were captured. The facilitator will also read through the parking lot items that captured important side conversations that were not relevant to the pull plan, and make sure a champion is assigned to set up a future meeting to review.

b. When trades have been dismissed, the facilitator needs to take photographs of all boards as documentation. Later, these dates will be added back into the master schedule and distributed to the trades weekly as a six-week schedule.

After the Pull Planning session:

a. It will take some time after the pull plan session to document the cards and incorporate the dates into the schedule. This should be done by the superintendent(s) and project management team working together. This should be completed within a few days so that no time or information is lost.

b. Once the master schedule has been updated with the pull plan schedule, the master schedule should be sent to all trade partners with the photographs of the pull plan cards to review for any questions or clarifications. If there are questions or concerns, it is good practice to hold a follow-up meeting to walk through the logic a final time.

c. The general contractor will issue a six-week look-ahead on a weekly basis which will allow the trade partners to fill out the *Three-Week Look-Ahead* board. The three-week look-ahead durations should tie back to the six-week look-ahead and pull plan commitments.

Look-Ahead Planning, mentioned in item C directly above, is the next step in the system. This allows the team to review the upcoming six weeks, every week.

As previously mentioned, after the pull plan the general contractor will update the master schedule with the activities and durations committed to by the last planners. When completed, the general contractor will issue a six-week look-ahead to the team. This gives the team a road map of the upcoming work and allows the last planners time to identify and clear constraints that might slow down or prevent upcoming work from being completed as planned.

The six-week schedule could be produced as a Gantt chart from scheduling software, or in Excel where you can break out work by trade, color code activities, add a constraint column, etc. It is important that the six-week look-ahead is updated with what is going on in the field, and that it is sent to the trades each week.

Weekly Work Planning, also known as commitment planning, will be the differentiating factor in your daily huddle meetings once the team is bought into the collaborative process. A *Three-Week Look-Ahead* board can be introduced into the daily huddle meeting as a dashboard tool to keep everyone on track. Recommendations on creating, filling out, and implementing your *Three-Week Look-Ahead* board are included below.

Creating the Three-Week Look-Ahead board

The benefit of making a visual *Three-Week Look-Ahead* board is that it will serve as a tool for helping everyone to be on the same page at the daily huddle. You can build your three-week calendar board in Excel with the following categories:

- Item #
- Activity/Work to be Done

- Manpower Tracking
- Scoring

The *Three-Week Look-Ahead* board can be printed on plotter paper or drawn onto a whiteboard; either way, it should be displayed where you will be having your daily huddles. This board will be next to your other visual communication tools, like your constraint board.

Filling out the Three-Week Look-Ahead board

The six-week look-ahead should be used as a guide while the last planners fill out the *Three-Week Look-Ahead* board.

- **Activities/Work to Be Done**

Last planners will fill out the *Activities/Work to be Done* section of the board with their designated dry erase marker color, breaking down their items in more detail than what is in the six-week look-ahead. They should only be writing activities on the board that release other work to begin.

The *Activities/Work to be Done* column is scored weekly, so it is critical to be specific as to what the commitment is for each week. If an activity spans ten days on the *Three-Week Look-Ahead* board, be sure that the commitment is clear that only fifty percent of the work will be complete in the first week.

Once the trades have written their activities on the board for the next three weeks, the superintendent should verify the following:

- if the activities listed are critical path activities, or activities that have handoffs to other trades; and
- if the activity is confirmed to be ready for execution.

Activities listed must be specific enough that work can be coordinated with other trades, and it is possible to tell by the end of the week whether the work has been complete or not.

- **Manpower Tracking**

Next to the *Activities/Work to be Done* column are the weeks/days columns for the next three weeks. These are used to track the expected manpower it will take for each task to be completed per day.

For example, if the activity is *Tape & bed level one,* and this takes *one week to complete,* and that requires *three workers per day, each day of the week,* then the trade partner can fill in this information accordingly by writing the activity and filling in a "3" in each box for the assigned week. Now the team can easily see and understand the task (tape and bed of level one), the duration (one week) and when it will occur, and that three people will be working each day to fulfill the commitment.

When the last planners are reviewing their activities at the huddle, it is important to ask how many men they have working that day to ensure it matches the plan. If the manpower level is substantially lower than the plan, this could be an early indicator that the commitment is not going to be met.

- **Constraints/Needs**

Not to be confused with the constraint board, the constraints/needs column on the *Three-Week Look-Ahead* board means that the upcoming work will be constrained to start if it is not addressed immediately. This column serves as a reminder to the team that there is an immediate impact looming.

Using the Three-Week Look-Ahead board

The Friday before your first daily huddle using the new *Three-Week Look-Ahead* board, have the trades come in one at a time throughout the day to fill out their activities, manpower tracking, and constraints on the board in their dry erase color. You should be reviewing what they populate on the board and be asking the following questions:

- Are all the activities workable?
- Will the team understand what is required?
- Will the team understand what is needed from others?
- Are activities achievable within the planned period?

If the answer is *No* to any of these questions, ask the trade partner to revise what has been written. When the board has been completely and correctly populated, you will be ready for Monday's daily huddle.

Every day at the huddle, ask each last planner to read *what activities they are working on* and state *what current manpower they have* for implementing it. Have them show the team on the visual communication board.

On Fridays, the last planners will reveal to the team if they met their commitments or not.

Scoring

The scoring columns are for confirming that the activities committed to have either been completed or not completed. On Friday's huddle, ask each last planner if the work they had committed to be completed for that week is either done or not. If the answer is *Yes*, a Y goes in the box; if the answer is *No*, then an N goes in the box. When grading the Weekly Work Plan to establish the PPC score, remember the answer is either *Yes* or *No* if the commitment was made; there is no gray area.

Everyone needs to be honest with the team as to why a commitment was not met in order to clearly identify the root cause. Once you understand the root cause, you can then begin to effectively correct the variation. (This is addressed later in this Playbook in *Percent Plan Complete*.)

The Wipe Down
When the meeting is over on Friday and the board has been scored, take a photo of the *Three-Week Look-Ahead* board for reference. Then wipe it down so the trades can come in throughout the day and populate the board for the next three weeks.

Use the data from that week to update your six-week look-ahead for the next six weeks. Then post the new six-week look-ahead and the photo of the previous three weeks up next to the three-week board for reference. Trades will begin the process again by coming in throughout the day to update the cleaned boards.

The **Percent Plan Complete (PPC)** portion of the Last Planner System is often overlooked by many project teams who think of the Last Planner System as an à la carte menu—selecting a little pull planning here and a little look-ahead planning there. However, the Last Planner System is not designed in this manner. It is a holistic system, and *Percent Plan Complete* happens to be one of the most important parts of the Last Planner System, as it is the learning opportunity, the chance to get better as a team and shore up the commitments to be more reliable. Below are a few items that might help you and your team implement PPC easily and effectively.

Creating the Percent Plan Complete (PPC) board
The benefit of making a visual *Percent Plan Complete* board is that it will serve as a tool for helping everyone to be on the same page at the daily huddle. You can build your *Percent Plan Complete* board with the following categories:

- Activities Completed
- Activities Promised
- Weekly Team Percentage
- Root Cause Categories
- Root Causes for Work Missed
- Twelve-Week Snapshot

The *Percent Plan Complete* board can be printed on plotter paper or drawn onto a whiteboard; either way, it should be displayed where you will be having your daily huddles. This board will be next to your other visual communication tools, like your constraint board.

Colored dry erase markers are needed to build the color-coded key of root causes for work that was not completed. Predetermined root causes for missed commitments are:

- weather;
- manpower;
- machinery;
- design;
- make-ready;
- materials;

- poor scheduling; and
- other.

Filling out & Implementing the Percent Plan Complete board

Weekly Team Percentage

After the last planners have been dismissed from Friday's huddle, tally up the *number of activities completed* and *divide by the number of the activities promised*. This will yield a percentage of commitments met.

Remember: the *Percent Plan Complete* score is not a reflection of production. It is the score of how well the team is making commitments to one another. This is an important lesson that will take some longer than others to learn.

Monitor the entire team's score per week rather than the individual trade partner scores. A high score is not necessarily good news; if your team's score is consistently in the mid- to high ninetieth percentile, the team is not challenging itself to an acceptable level.

Root Causes

Knowing the weekly percentage of commitments that the team has made is a great metric, but understanding the reasons—the root causes—for the missed commitments is more important.

A root cause pie chart on the *Percent Plan Complete* board can be a great way to understand what categories these root causes are coming from. Add a circle to your board, and divide the *number of root cause types* by the *number of missed commitments*, and you will have the root cause percentage by type. This could help identify trends on the project such as manpower shortages, slow design response times, and weather impacts.

Having the last planners take accountability and discuss the root cause for missing a commitment can be tough at first. Typically, there is a lot of noise around things not getting completed in the field, but with the Last Planner System and *Percent Plan Complete*, there is nowhere to hide.

It is one thing to identify the root cause; it is another to do something about it. After the Friday huddle is over, the general contractor can follow up on every commitment missed with an email, phone call, or both. For example, if there is an RFI that is delaying work and the root cause is *design*, there is a call to the design team followed up with an email to try to resolve the issue.

Twelve-Week Snapshot
The twelve-week snapshot portion of the board allows the team to see how the commitments percentage has been tracking over a period of time. This is a great metric to see how the team had trended over the life cycle of a project and how that team progressed or regressed.

Each week, the PPC board will be wiped down and the weekly team percentage and root cause pie chart will change, but the twelve-week snapshot will show via a line graph the percentage score for all to see.

Implementation
Remember, you will score the *Three-Week Look-Ahead* activities on Fridays and ask last planners for the root cause for missed

work. Upon completion of the huddle, you will carry over that information to the *Percent Plan Complete* board and fill out:

1. activities completed/activities promised;
2. weekly team percentage;
3. root causes pie chart; and
4. twelve-week snapshot.

This information will be reviewed with the team at the Monday daily huddle.

RefinemySite – The Lean Builder

Appendix

If you're like us, at some point you'll want to know which digital tools might simplify the work of last planners while helping them to be better planners and builders. While the effort required by the Last Planner System® produces fewer coordination conflicts and reduces other wastes, the Lean mindset is centered around continuous improvement: always looking for ways to improve how all work is done.

RefinemySite by Bosch is a digital Last Planner System collaboration platform that addresses many of the challenges with the "sticky note approach" to managing Look-Ahead Planning, Weekly Work Planning, Daily Huddles, and Percent Plan Complete learning. It's also a tool that can be used to document your Master and Phase planning sessions. It's intuitive and easy to use. The field and project management team members enter the pull plan into **Refine**mySite—and this can be done quickly, even during the pull planning meeting, so last planners have the completed plan that same day.

It's also versatile. Last planners can use **Refine**mySite on their computers, phones, and tablets. This makes it easy for them to have daily huddles in the field, and to review their work plans with their crews. The digital format also allows them to record information about their work, including photos. Using the voice-to-text feature makes using **Refine**mySite even easier. And no more walking back to the field office, where space is limited, to check on what other trades are doing each day.

Your time spent managing your project decreases, and gathering your tasks digitally adds transparency and benefits your entire team.

RefinemySite has been used on hundreds of projects, ranging from small to very large. It is backed up by Bosch, a leading provider of quality power tools and connected devices, whose goal is to provide software and hardware solutions to connect people and processes with relevant technology to create an end-to-end Lean construction ecosystem. Think of **Refine**mySite as a digital power tool for the Last Planner System.

The bottom line is **Refine**mySite is simple to use and provides the best platform for new and experienced last planners to learn and apply the Last Planner System. And it is affordable. We're all tired of software that charges us for every person we add to the project. With **Refine**mySite, you add as many people as you want without paying more money—and the price you pay is more affordable than any other Last Planner System digital tool that's available.

If you want to learn more about **Refine**mySite by Bosch, scan the QR code below to visit a webpage they built especially for readers of *The Lean Builder*.

The bulk of The Playbook is devoted to teaching the Last Planner System®, but we think understanding "The Eight Deadly Wastes" and how they can adversely impact your project's schedule, budget, and morale are important; and so, we're including an explanation of this concept here as well.

BONUS:
The Eight Wastes

Waste can be defined as *any task that does not add value*.

Unfortunately for the construction industry, many of the activities performed in the design and construction industry are non-value-added activities, or *waste*.

The first step to overcoming the wasteful issues that plague your jobsite is being able to recognize and identify The Eight Wastes. This empowers you to pinpoint the root cause of your issues much faster, thereby allowing you to resolve constraints and challenges more effectively without getting sidetracked by the noise surrounding the issues.

Acronyms provide an easy way to remember the categories for the Eight Wastes, and there are several acronyms that different people use to describe what these wastes are; one of the more common ones is DOWNTIME.

"The Eight Deadly Wastes of a Jobsite," as described using the DOWNTIME acronym, are:

Defects
Materials that have been damaged or made incorrectly, or work that needs to be repaired, replaced, or redone due to mistakes, are all known as *defects*.

Overproduction
Building something too soon, having too much of something already built, or building something quicker than it is needed. It is important to produce and deliver the right amount of material at the time it is needed.

Waiting
Delays, or periods of inactivity. Work that is not able to be performed due to the impact(s) from other waste(s) can be considered *waiting*. When trades are idle in anticipation of the delivery of material, equipment, completion of preceding activities, or information (such as a submittal or RFI), *waiting* will occur.

Non-Utilized Talent
Inadequate or improper use of people's skills, resourcefulness, or knowledge on your jobsite. A project's people are its greatest advantage; it is important that they are focused on the activities that create value.

Transportation
Unnecessary movement of materials or equipment. Movement from one area, floor, or material laydown space and then to the area where it will be put in place is *transportation* waste. This waste cannot be eliminated, but it is important to recognize how it can

add time and cost to your project, and could lead to damages (*defects*), thereby causing you to lose more time and/or money.

Inventory
Overproduction that results in excess. *Inventory* can be material being stored on your floors, in your laydown yard, or offsite. Maintaining some *inventory* onsite may be required to keep the project progressing; however, too much *inventory* can quickly add up, and tie up money and other resources. All *inventory* will involve extra handling and storage space.

Motion
Movement by craftsman. To move and add value is called work; to move and not add value is called *motion*. Even what seems like a small non-value-added *motion* can cost your project; and multiple *motions* add up. Craftsman having to spend time looking for a tool or a set of current plans, or walking extra yards due to poorly placed port-a-johns, are all examples of *motion*.

Excess
The redundant steps taken in a process (also called over-processing), such as handling supplies or materials multiple times, or having to alter them. *Excess* is often incorporated into a process as an outcome of *defects, overproduction,* and excess *inventory.* Examples of *excess* in construction include administrative paperwork such as double data entry, multiple signatures on forms, redundant daily logs, or forwarding emails with drawings and RFIs.

Equipping last planners to identify the Eight Wastes and understand their root causes is an essential first step towards shifting your jobsite or company culture. In just a few hours of training, last planners can begin to shift the lens in which they see waste on their jobsite or in their organization, allowing them the awareness to begin generating ideas on how to reduce or eliminate each one that comes across their path. This fundamental step is the essence of the Lean philosophy and the heart of continuous improvement.

Continue Your Journey

Are you ready to keep "sharpening your axe"?
More information, support, and resources
can be found on our website:

www.theleanbuilder.com

Join our mailing list and stay up to date on our
podcasts, workshops, and blog posts.

Or, feel free to get in touch with us by email:

joe@theleanbuilder.com
keyan@theleanbuilder.com

About the Authors

Joe Donarumo serves as Vice President – Field Operations for Linbeck in Fort Worth, TX, where he has been able to develop and lead high-performing field teams across multiple healthcare projects. Joe has a unique passion for Lean implementation, continuous improvement, and a ruthless pursuit of waste elimination within his projects and organization. Joe lives in Aledo, TX with his wife Tasha, their three sons, Karsten, Kaiser, and Knox, and their daughter, Krosby.

Keyan Zandy is a longtime Lean practitioner, enthusiast, and advocate. As Skiles Group's CEO, he has a dual focus on client service and on nurturing a progressive company culture, and is ultimately responsible for the oversight of the firm's daily operations. Keyan lives in Fairview, TX, with his wife, Tere, and their two sons, Marshall and Calvin.